The Sixth Armada Ghost Book

This Armada book belongs to:

_____

_____

_____

The Sixth Armada Ghost Book

Edited by Mary Danby

Armada

The Sixth Armada Ghost Book was first
published in the U.K. in 1974 by
William Collins Sons & Co. Ltd.,
14 St James's Place, London S.W.1.

Second impression 1974

Printed in Great Britain by
Love & Malcomson Ltd., Brighton Road,
Redhill, Surrey.

CONTENTS

ACKNOWLEDGEMENTS

THE editor gratefully acknowledges permission to reprint copyright material to the following:

Ruth Ainsworth and Andre Deutsch Ltd., for MIRROR MIRROR ON THE WALL (from "The Phantom Cyclist and Other Stories"). © Ruth Ainsworth 1971.

Kay Leith for MACKRIN MAINS. © Kay Leith 1974

Pat Klacar for THE GHOST WITH A LONG MEMORY. © Pat Klacar 1974.

Terry Gisbourne for COBWEBS. © Terry Gisbourne 1974.

Mary Clarke for SPLENDID ANCESTOR. © Mary Clarke 1974.

Christine Pullein-Thompson for ISOBEL'S PONY. © Christine Pullein-Thompson 1974.

Louise Francke for ALICIA. © Louise Francke 1974.

James Turner and Hughes Massie Ltd., for THE MODEL (first published in "Spectre 1"). © James Turner 1973.

Sydney J. Bounds for ROOM AT THE INN. © Sydney J. Bounds 1974.

EDWARD (first published in "Spectre 1"). © Mary Danby 1973.

INTRODUCTION

WHAT does a ghost look like? A misty, moaning phantom, with filmy bits round the edges? A chain-rattling horror with its head under its arm? Or the man across the street— a flesh-and-blood person, as solid as you and me.

If you are not sure whether someone is a ghost, you can try the mirror test, for they say that a ghost has no reflection. But can you be *sure*, even then? In Ruth Ainsworth's *Mirror Mirror on the Wall*, Jane sees the reflection of a long-dead child. But is she seeing a ghost, or is Jane herself travelling into the past? Is she, in fact, a ghost of the future?

Mackrin Mains tells the story of an old, remote house and a family who find themselves unwelcome visitors—the targets of an ancient and terrible revenge. And another visitor in trouble is the shady Mr. Ibbotson, when he encounters *The Ghost with a Long Memory*. Her name is Serena, but the sight of Mr. Ibbotson sets her whiskers twitching in a most un-serene manner!

Two children, a castle, a weeping woman and a vault of gold—these are the ingredients of *Cobwebs*, while *Splendid Ancestor* is the story of a girl and a portrait which is more than just paint and canvas. . . .

Christine Pullein-Thomson (remember her grippingly spooky tale of *The Skeleton Rider* in the 5th Armada Ghost Book?) tells the mysterious story of *Isobel's Pony*. Why does the pony come back, night after night, to haunt Isobel's sleep with his eerie neighing? The answer lies in the dark, murderous past.

Attics are usually the resting-places of old pictures, suitcases, pieces of furniture and centuries of junk. *Alicia* knows about the rocking-chair in her attic. It hasn't been used for years. But one day, one dreadful day, she finds someone sitting in it. . . .

There's something else you might see in an attic—an old dolls' house. Perhaps with the tiny figures still inside, stiff and silent, mere puppets. But are they? How three inhabitants of a dolls' house come to life and relive a grim tragedy is told with chilling tension in *The Model*. And another scene from a long-gone age appears to threaten Jane and Penny with a gruesome fate when they find a *Room at the Inn* on the bleak wastes of Bodmin Moor.

Edward is my own contribution to this book. I can only say I hope it sends a few tingling fingers up your spine.

Ten ghostly tales. Some may scare you, some may amuse you. All of them, I hope, will haunt you.

MARY DANBY

MIRROR MIRROR ON THE WALL

by Ruth Ainsworth

IN winter, a heavy blue curtain was drawn across the front door to keep out the draughts. A little girl named Jane liked to hide behind it. There was nothing and no one to hide from. No one was playing hide-and-seek with her, or looking for her. But she hid there because she chose to.

As Jane crouched behind the soft velvet curtain, she could draw the edge a little to one side, and peep out. By doing this, she saw the gilt-framed mirror in the hall, which reflected a little of the hall itself, and half of the flight of stairs. The mirror looked so beautiful, like a pool of clear water, and the stairs looked beautiful too, painted white, with dark blue carpet to walk on.

She could also see, if she leaned out, the edge of the curtain and her hand holding it. She looked very pale and small in the mirror, and her hair looked very fair. She looked much paler and smaller and fairer than she really was.

Without moving the curtain she could see her mother going up or down stairs, and she could see her father when he came home from work. He always came in at the back door as it was nearer to the garage. Her mother met him in the hall and kissed him. She always said: "Had a good day, dear?"

And he always replied; "Quite good, but busy."

When her cousin Maggie came to stay, they both hid behind the curtain, but Maggie soon got tired of being there.

9

"This curtain suffocates me," she cried. "Let's jump out at your mother when she comes into the hall, and give her a fright. Or we'll wait and jump out at your father. That will be fun."

"I don't want to," said Jane. "If we do that, they'll know where we are, and I like my hiding places to be kept secret."

"Oh, please yourself," said Maggie crossly. "I'm going to ride your rocking horse."

Jane watched her in the mirror, running upstairs in her scarlet tights. Maggie hadn't a rocking horse at home and she was never tired of riding on Jane's. He had black spots and a red bridle and saddle. He had gleaming black eyes, too, and a black mane.

Jane liked playing with Maggie, but she did not mind when she went home. Then she could go back to hiding in peace, looking into the mirror where everything was the same, yet different.

One evening, when Jane was behind the curtain, she felt a little bit sleepy. Perhaps it was rather stuffy behind its soft folds. As she looked out at the gilt-framed mirror the glass clouded over in an odd way. When the glass cleared, she saw somebody, not her mother, going up the stairs. It was a strange woman in a white apron, with a white cap on her head. She was dragging a little boy by the hand, a little boy about Jane's age.

"Now come along," said the woman sharply. "It's past your bedtime. Don't make such a to-do, Master Abel. I'm ashamed of you."

"But I wanted to see Polly have her calf. Jones said it would be by morning. I wanted to see if it would be black and white like Polly, or all white like its father."

"Oh fie, Master Abel, the byre is no place for you. No wonder you're all plastered with mud. Now come along, or I shan't leave the candle alight when I say good-night."

This mild threat had an instant effect on the little boy. He stopped pulling and followed the woman quietly upstairs. He was wearing a little striped jacket with a lace collar, and long, striped trousers. His shoes had silver buckles on them.

"Poor Abel," thought Jane. "He's afraid of the dark as I used to be. I remember always having my bedroom door ajar, and crying if anyone switched off the landing light by mistake. I wonder why I don't mind now?"

Then she saw her father come in and greet her mother, and she slipped out of her hiding place and ran into the sitting-room to kiss him.

"Have you ever heard of a boy called Abel?" she asked.

"Only in the Bible," said her father.

"I met one today," said Jane.

"Do you mean at school?"

"No. Not at school. In the looking glass."

"You mean you heard a story about Abel?"

"Not exactly, Daddy. Let's play one game of halma before I go to bed. We'll just have time. You can be yellow and I'll be red."

A few nights later Jane saw Abel again, when she was in her hiding place. He was wearing the same striped suit and lace collar, and he was having another tussle with the woman in the white cap and apron.

"No, Master Abel, you can't take your hobbyhorse upstairs. It's not meant to go into your bedchamber. You've been riding it outside and it's muddy."

"But I love my hobbyhorse, Patty, and I want it to stand beside my bed. I won't get to sleep if I can't have it."

"Then you'll have to stay awake, won't you?" Patty snatched the horse from his grasp and dropped it down the stairs. Jane had a good view of it as it fell. It was a stick with a wooden horse's head on one end, and a bridle. It had bells somewhere because she heard them jingle.

11

"Poor Abel," she thought again. "How cross Patty seems. I wish he had someone like my mummy to put him to bed. She wouldn't mind his having his horse in his bedroom. When I wanted my new tricycle to be near my bed she asked Daddy to bring it up from the garage."

When her father came home the mirror just reflected the stairs and hall as usual. She didn't ask any more questions about Abel. She kept him a secret, like the hiding place behind the curtain.

The next time Abel appeared, the scene was different. Jane had felt sleepy and the mirror had clouded over as before, when suddenly it cleared. She saw a man carrying something carefully in his arms. Patty followed behind, crying bitterly.

"He's dead," she sobbed. "He's dead."

"Now don't distress yourself," said the man. "His new pony threw him and kicked him between the eyes and he's in a swoon. Brown has ridden off for the physician. We must get him to bed and put a hot brick at his feet, and try to stop the bleeding with cold compresses."

"Poor little chap," said Patty. "I knew he was too young to ride that strong, nervous pony, but his father is so anxious for him to be manly."

"Manly indeed!" said the man. "He's a long way off being a man, poor bairn. Now make haste with the compresses while I lay him on the bed. He's losing a deal of blood."

Jane was horrified. Would Abel die? Would the physician come soon? Where was his mother? Everything seemed so slow. Why couldn't they have telephoned?

She stayed behind the curtain till she heard her father call out:

"Where's Jane?"

Her mother answered:

12

"Oh, playing around. She's always disappearing after tea. I think it's a kind of game. She's up to no harm."

Jane slipped out from behind the curtain and ran to her father.

"How's Abel today?" he asked, half teasing.

"He's very very ill. His pony kicked him."

"I believe you just make up stories about Abel."

"He *is* in a story, in a way. But it's not my story."

"Shall we have a game of halma?"

"All right."

Jane fetched the board and the counters but she was thinking all the while of something else. She forgot when it was her turn and didn't see when there was a good move to be made. Her father won easily.

"You're a tired girl tonight," he said, as he kissed her. "A very tired girl."

Perhaps Jane was tired because she fell asleep soon after her mother turned out the light. At first she began to think about Abel, but her thoughts ran together in a jumble and then faded away. She slept deeply, without dreaming or moving. There was hardly a wrinkle in the bedclothes when, suddenly she was awake. She had changed in a second from being deeply asleep to being absolutely wide awake.

Something had waked her, she was sure, but what? It was pitch dark and it must be very late because the landing light was turned off. That meant that her parents had gone to bed. She sat up and listened.

At first all was silent. Then she heard a low, moaning sound. She knew at once that it was a child crying quietly; a child trying not to cry. She got out of bed and put on her dressing-gown and slippers, and started to walk down the passage. She passed the door of her parents' room. The bathroom. The spare room. Then she came to the playroom. The door had changed completely. Instead of

She lifted the iron latch . . .

being painted white, it was of some dark wood, with a heavy iron latch. She lifted the iron latch and went in.

The room had changed, too. Her rocking-horse had gone, and her dolls' house, and all her other toys. The gas fire had gone, too. A coal fire was burning in the grate, and there was a rocking-chair by the fire in which Patty was sitting. She was fast asleep, wrapped in a grey shawl, and snoring slightly. But Jane had no time to attend to Patty. Against the wall was a bed hung with curtains, and in this bed lay Abel, white as chalk, with a broad bandage across his forehead, covering his eyes. Jane tiptoed to his side and took one of his hot hands in hers.

"Is it very bad?" she whispered.

"Yes, it's pretty bad. I tried not to make a din and wake Patty."

"Oughtn't she to be awake, and taking care of you?"

"She's tired out. She needs some sleep."

"Where is your mother?"

"My mother died when I was a baby."

"And your father?"

"My father is at the war. He is a soldier, a captain, and rides a great black horse. He's the best captain in the army, and the bravest."

"You're brave too," said Jane. "I should be crying much worse if my pony had kicked me. I'd be screaming. I screamed and screamed when I shut my finger in the door and my nail came off."

"Well, you're a girl. You don't need to be brave. You'll never have to go to the war and fight. But who are you? I've never seen you before."

"I'm Jane. I've seen you before. I saw you in the mirror."

"I don't understand. My head aches so much."

"I don't understand either. Is your head very bad?"

"No, not so *very* bad. I was crying because Master

15

Pepys, the physician, said I might lose my sight. I'd rather die than go blind."

"But Abel, if he said you might lose your sight then it's just as likely that you might not. Let's believe that you'll not be blind."

"All right, I'll try."

"Do your eyes hurt?"

"No. Caesar's hoof struck my brow, but Master Pepys said some nerve might be damaged. He didn't think I heard what he said. He was talking to Patty."

Patty stirred and the rocking-chair creaked.

"I'll go now," whispered Jane.

"Come and see me tomorrow, please come."

"I'll come tomorrow if I can. And I'll think of you. I'll wish for your eyes to be all right."

She lifted the latch as quietly as she could, and went back to bed. The bed was still warm and she snuggled down under the clothes. She meant to think about Abel and the strange room and the coal fire, but she fell asleep instead.

The next thing she knew was that her mother was gently shaking her.

"I've let you sleep on, darling, and it's now ten o'clock. You must have been terribly tired. Do you feel quite well?"

Her mother put a cool hand on her forehead.

"I'm quite well, Mummy. I feel absolutely well." And Jane jumped out of bed, dressed in a twinkling, and ate an extra large breakfast to prove it.

"There's nothing much wrong," said her mother, cutting Jane another slice of bread and honey. "You'd better go back to school this afternoon and I'll send a note to explain why you missed this morning."

That evening Jane did not hide behind the curtain and watch the gilt-framed mirror. She was sure there would be nothing special to see, only ordinary things. But she thought about Abel all the time, and hoped she would be able to see him that night.

Again, she slept deeply, and woke suddenly in the middle of the night. There was no sound of muffled crying this time. All was silent. She put on her dressing-gown and slippers and went along the landing, past the familiar white doors, until she came to the heavy wooden one with the iron latch. Gently as she could, she lifted the latch and went in.

Patty was asleep in the rocking-chair and the fire was glowing a dull red. A candle burned on the mantelpiece. She walked to the bedside and looked down at Abel. His face was still white with the bandage covering the upper part.

"Is it you, Jane?" he whispered, as she stood looking down.

"Yes, it's me. How are you?"

"I feel better, but I mustn't move—not even to turn over in bed. I'm very weary. The hours seem like weeks."

"You poor boy. I wish I could come and visit you in the daytime, but—but I don't know how. I only know the way in the night. Shall I tell you a story? Do you like exciting ones?"

"Thank you, Jane, but I'd rather talk."

"Yes, so would I."

Having decided to talk, at first they neither of them had anything to say.

"Do you go to school?" said Jane.

"Not yet. But I may go soon."

"Then do you play all day, like I do in the holidays?"

"No indeed. I have a tutor, Dr. Wynd. He teaches me Latin and Greek."

"How clever you must be! I shan't do Latin till I'm much older, perhaps twelve or thirteen, and I don't suppose I shall ever learn Greek. Say some Latin to me. I want to know what it sounds like."

"Facta non verba," said Abel.

"Whatever does that mean?"

"Deeds, not words."

"What else does Dr. Wynd teach you?"

"Why, nothing. But I shall do some mathematics at school."

"Will you like school?"

"No, I shall hate it. Here I have my dogs and my pony and the estate to roam about in. I shall lose my freedom. And Dr. Wynd is gentle with me. The ushers at school are very strict."

"But you'll enjoy the games," said Jane.

"What games?"

"Why, cricket and football and swimming."

"I've never heard of cricket and football, but I can swim here in the river with the village boys. Or I could if I was allowed. Tell me about your school."

Jane told him all she could about her school, and the games they played at break, and how they played rounders. Abel could hardly believe that the children at Jane's school painted, and sang, and made things out of clay.

"We have fun," went on Jane. "We dress up and act plays, and it's lovely having stories. Doesn't Dr. Wynd teach you to read and write?"

"Oh, I could do that before he came. The priest taught me. I could read and write when I was four."

"Four!" exclaimed Jane. "I'm six and I can only just read and write easy words."

"Then you're a great dunce," said Abel.

"I'm not. I'm just like everyone else. How do your eyes feel?"

"I don't know. I try to open them under the bandage, but it's all dark."

18

"Of course it's dark under the bandage. It's like blind man's buff."

"Oh, do you play that too?" said Abel.

They were both pleased that they had something in common, if it was only "blind man's buff".

The logs in the fire settled with a slight noise. Patty moved her head.

"I must go now," whispered Jane. "I'll see you to-morrow."

The next evening Jane asked her father about the mirror in the hall.

"I don't know much about it," said her father, "except that it's old. It was Granny's once."

"Where did she get it from?"

"I think it was her mother's. I believe your great-grand-father bought it at a sale. He had a good eye for antiques. Do you like it?"

"I like it better than anything else in the whole house."

"I didn't know you were so vain," said her father.

"Oh, I don't look at myself in it, or hardly ever. I look at other people. It's so beautiful."

Jane got into the way of visiting Abel every night. She was always sleepy in the morning, but not as sleepy as she had been the first time. Once Patty was bending over the black kettle that stood on the fire, making a drink, and Jane withdrew. Once Abel was so fast asleep that she did not try to disturb him. But usually he heard her tiptoe in.

Then, one night, she found the door open and the chair by the fire empty.

"Patty has gone to sleep in her own chamber," said Abel. "I can ring if there is anything I want."

There was a little bell beside his bed, within easy reach.

"That's good. Then I can stay longer and we needn't whisper all the time."

They found many things to talk about, though Jane

found that certain words puzzled Abel, and made him uneasy. If she mentioned the telephone or television, or said that her father had flown to Italy, he looked worried, almost frightened. She soon learned to avoid these words and they talked about books and pets and the garden. His garden was different from the one she played in, but both had an oak tree near the gate. They both knew Mr. Hutchinson's farm.

"It belongs to my father," said Abel.

"I think it belongs to Mr. Hutchinson now," said Jane.

"Why do you say 'now'?" asked Abel.

"I don't know. It just slipped out. Of course it's always 'now' when we're together. It must be."

One night Abel greeted Jane with the news that in two days the bandage was to be removed from his eyes.

"Then you'll see."

"Then I may see," corrected Abel.

"You will see. I'll keep my fingers crossed for you."

The next night Jane said to Abel:

"Hold out your hand. It's something nice, I promise."

She put something very tiny into it.

"What is it, Jane?"

"It's my lucky four-leafed clover leaf. I've had it for ages. I found it at Granny's."

"Oh thank you."

"Where will you put it to keep it safe?"

"I'll put it in my Bible, where the marker is."

The next night Jane's heart was beating fast as she opened Abel's door. The candle was burning on the mantelpiece, and she ran quickly to the bedside. A pair of large dark brown eyes looked up at her.

"Then it's all right? You can see me?"

"Yes, it's all right. I've got to be careful but I shan't be blind. Let me give you back your four-leafed clover."

"No, keep it. Perhaps it will help you to like school after all."

A few nights later Jane had difficulty in finding the heavy wooden door. She wandered up and down the passage almost in tears, when suddenly she found it, and lifted the latch and went in.

"I was ages finding you tonight, Abel. Ages and ages. What is happening?"

"I don't know, but don't give up coming to see me."

"Oh I won't—unless I have to."

A week or so later Jane could not find the door anywhere. She found her own playroom, with its white door and the rocking-horse and the dolls' house, but the wooden door had vanished. She went back to bed and cried. In a moment her father was beside her, holding her in his arms.

"What is it, darling? A bad dream?"

"I—I couldn't find something. I couldn't find somebody. I'm lost, Daddy, I'm lost."

"It was a bad dream, but you're awake now. There's nothing to cry about."

"But there is, you don't understand. There's everything to cry about."

Her father stayed beside her, stroking her hair, till she fell asleep.

Jane felt that she'd never see Abel again. His room had vanished and when she peered into the gilt-framed mirror there were only ordinary things to see, the hall, the white staircase, and her father and mother. Nothing more.

Then, after she'd given up hope, she saw Abel just once more. The nights were getting lighter, and it was on her way up to bed that she stopped to look in the mirror. She felt sleepy. The glass clouded over, and then it cleared. There was Abel, in a dark hat and coat, and Patty, and a man carrying a box.

21

"You'll be all right," said Patty gently. "Brown will ride with you to the turnpike and put you on the coach. It'll only be a few months before you are home again."

"You'll like school," said Brown. "You'll get up to mischief with the other young gentlemen, I'll be bound."

But Jane could see by Abel's face that he was on the verge of tears.

"Patty," he said, as she kissed him, "care for my rabbits and talk to Caesar sometimes. Don't let him forget me."

"I'll do that, Master Abel. Never fear."

Jane sprang from behind the curtain and ran out, catching Abel's arm.

"I'll write to you," she said, "really I will. And you must write to me. Where is your school? What's the address?"

At once a look of surprise, almost horror, came over the faces of Patty and Brown. Abel smiled and began to speak, but no words came except a faint "farewell".

She was alone in the hall. She looked in the mirror and knew that she would never see Abel again. She could no longer get back into that other world.

She breathed on the glass and made a misty patch. She wrote an "A" in the mist with her finger. But it soon faded. She went slowly up to bed, the mirror reflecting her bowed, fair head.

MACKRIN MAINS

by Kay Leith

"THERE isn't even a hint of another house. There's just nothing for miles and miles but hills and trees and heather. There are trout streams and marshy places. The house is two-storied—combe-ceilings upstairs—and although the stonework is all right, the woodwork is terrible and there are lots of slates missing from the roof."

Sylvia wondered if her mother was pitching it too strong, and bit back the words that threatened to spill out and spoil everything. They had agreed to paint the picture as it really was: no romantic frills, and no displays of gleeful enthusiasm.

That Sunday expedition, whilst her father had finished off his latest canvas in preparation for his summer exhibition, had borne fruit. The search had taken months. They had seen so many houses which were either out of their price range, or were too near to other houses and therefore did not come within their terms of reference. It was not that they intended to abandon civilization—they merely wanted a little less of it.

"What's the decorative condition?" asked Colin.

"Decorative condition!" snorted Maggie. "What wallpaper there was has fallen off because of the damp. I'm not sure about the colour of the last coat of paint, because it's discoloured where it hasn't actually peeled away. I assure you, apart from the stonework, it's a mess."

Sylvia's heart sank. Her mother had gone too far and killed the whole idea. But her father, strangely enough, appeared to be more interested just because they weren't trying to blind him with its advantages.

"You say there aren't any other houses for miles . . ." he mused.

"Oh, yes," said Maggie grudgingly, darting a sly twinkle at Sylvia. "It has that in its favour. It's isolated, all right. No doubt about that. But nobody could live there until the roof has been repaired."

"The joists—what about the joists?"

"From what I could see through the trapdoor, which wasn't much, they seem all right."

Colin flung down his paint brush and got up from the easel. He stared, first at Maggie, then at Sylvia, and shook his head in puzzlement. "I can't understand it. It sounds just what we've been looking for, so why aren't the pair of you all agog and singing its praises?"

Sylvia shot a glance at her mother, apologetically, traitorously. "I like it, Dad."

Colin sat down again. "Well, that's something, at any rate."

"And I like it, too," admitted Maggie, grinning.

"Well?"

His wife spread deprecating hands. "It's just that we don't want to pressure you into agreeing to take the house. There's so much that requires to be done to make it habitable, and we just don't have the money to pay somebody to do it for us. It would mean a great deal of hard work."

"What about water and electricity?"

"There's a well with a pump, but no electricity."

"Hmmm. . . ."

Maggie sighed. "Perhaps we ought to forget about it."

Just then the thunderous roar of the motorbike belonging to the boy downstairs drowned out all thought. This was followed by the crash of a door, the thud of feet on the stairs, and the shouts of children.

Maggie's and Colin's eyes met, and an unspoken decision was arrived at. Sylvia gave a quiet smile. Their ability to read each other's minds was sometimes uncanny.

Sylvia remembered the first time she had noticed it. They had gone to the zoo. It was very hot, and they paused to rest at a bench. Without speaking, her father rose and walked off. Sylvia looked up at her mother questioningly, but the latter did not seem concerned.

24

"Where has Dad gone?"

Her mother smiled, slightly astonished. "Didn't you hear him say that he was going to buy some ice cream?"

"But Dad didn't say anything——"

"Oh yes, he did. I distinctly heard him."

It became a family joke—a game. Sylvia found it quite easy when she concentrated. The three of them were so close that they were unable to decide whether they really had telepathic powers, or whether, because they knew each other so well, divining each other's thoughts and wishes was a natural ability, and was available to any-one willing to work at it.

They left Glasgow before dawn next day and gained their first glimpse of the purple ridges of the Monadhliath mountains at about eleven o'clock.

"There's a small signpost on the right when we go over a hump-back bridge," said Sylvia. "It says 'To Lochan Luoghair', or something like that."

"Yes," agreed her mother. "And we turn right there and carry on till we come to an old tree."

"Shall we stop and drink our coffee now? I'm parched."

"Oh, no, Colin. We're so near now. Let's wait till we get there."

On each side of the narrow road were fields with barren, rock-strewn earth and clumps of rowan and birch. There was the occasional stone-built cottage, and once they passed the high walls and wrought-iron gates of what must have been a large mansion, but all they could see of it was one crenellated turret above the surrounding trees.

"Look," said Colin. "It has a light at the gate, which means that there is electricity up to this point at any rate. Is it much farther?"

"Only another four or five miles—not far," said Maggie excitedly. "Here's the bridge."

"And there's the little signpost. Turn right here, Dad!" Sylvia wound down her window and breathed in the clean, sharp air. The last week in March, it was still chilly in the early morning and late evening, but during the day when the sun had had a chance to warm the air, it was pleasant. There was still snow on the peaks of the distant mountains, however.

To the left now was a heather-covered hill, to the right a small pine wood. Beyond a gnarled old alder a track led off—an overgrown track which must, in rainy weather, have been a treacherous river of mud.

The car bumped and lurched slowly up the track for what seemed miles, but was, in fact, quite a short distance, before the broken down, dry stone-walling of the garden of the house became visible.

The house itself stood high, as though the builder had specially chosen the site for its eminence. On closer inspection, however, it seemed to have been constructed on a circular platform of stones. The garden dropped away from the front door in a series of steps.

The wooden gate sagged drunkenly, finally collapsing altogether when Colin tried to push it open to make way for the car.

Finally, there they were, inside in the musty silence of the gloomy house. There was a large front room to the right, on the left a smaller room, and the passage led directly to the large kitchen at the back, with its huge iron range. The air was more damply cold there, seeming to strike through clothing and flesh to chill even one's bones.

Colin, coffee cup in hand, walked from room to room examining the flooring; then he made his way upstairs to check the first floor and the roof.

Sylvia found some dry wood and piled it in the kitchen fireplace, but the flames flickered only fitfully, then snuffed out, as though they found the grate too cold. She felt a curious, lonely dread, and went in search of her mother, who, after much frustrated pumping, was eventually rewarded by a gush of clear, cool water from the pump outside the kitchen door.

"I suppose it would have to be boiled until your father managed to check the drainage," she said, turning to Sylvia. "Well, darling, do you still like it?"

The girl grinned and nodded. "Oh, yes, Mum."

"You would have to stay with Gran in Glasgow during term-time."

That thought had already occurred to Sylvia. There didn't seem to be any way round the problem—unless a suitable school could be found for her in the neighbourhood. The only one they had passed was miles away and had only two classrooms!

"May I have the little room on the left at the top of the stairs?" she begged.

Maggie laughed. "We don't know yet whether your father will share our enthusiasm for the place, but if he does, the room's yours."

There was a fearsome rumbling, as though the whole place were falling to pieces, and a slate crashed into the front garden.

"That's not a very good sign," gasped Maggie, dashing upstairs, followed closely by Sylvia, to find her husband jumping from the trap door on the landing. "Colin, are you all right?"

"Yes, yes. Don't fuss!" He dusted himself off and straightened up.

"Well?" demanded Maggie.

"The place has distinct possibilities. I'll go in to Inverness now and put down a deposit."

Maggie clapped her hands with relief. "Oh, I'm so glad!"

"Whee-oo!" yipped Sylvia, jumping up and down and making the floor boards rattle. "Oh, how exciting! Please hurry, Dad, before somebody else decides to buy it."

Husband and wife burst out laughing. "I think it's been empty too long for much danger of that," reasoned Colin.

"We'd better come with you, darling," said Maggie. "It will save your having to come back here."

"Oh, Mum, let's stay a bit longer. There's so much to see," begged Sylvia.

"Oh, all right," agreed Maggie.

"I'll come back for you after I've seen the agent," said Colin. "I'll bring some food with me and we can picnic here."

As the car drove off, bumping and lurching, mother and daughter went off to explore the mouldering farm buildings. There was an air of eternity about everything, something which willed that no matter how many changes were made by man, there would always be a reversion, a return, to an ageless mossiness.

Later, they stood in the weed-infested front garden and looked at the house—the dirty paintwork, the washed-out, once white-rendered stones of the walls. A previous owner had planted sweet peas, which had seeded themselves time and again over the years and had eventually returned to their original pale purple. A stunted lilac tree would obviously not flower that year, and sickly green lichen threatened to choke the few live twigs of a raspberry bush.

"We'll root out all these weeds and put some fertilizer in the soil. The house will look crisp and clean when . . ." Maggie's voice trailed away and she passed a hand over her forehead, as though she had forgotten what she was going to say. She frowned and looked round, as though she had heard something.

A little worm of fear wriggled in Sylvia's mind, and the sky seemed to cloud over as the air grew still and bitingly cold. Bewildered, she saw her mother sway, as though pulled this way and that by unseen hands, and when she looked at the house she saw that the whitewash was gleaming and the clean windows had curtains on them. The roof was whole, and above it the sky sat leaden, like a predatory beast.

The red-painted door stood invitingly open, the iron shoe-scrapers shining with blacking. Her mother, strangely dressed in crude homespun, was walking slowly to the door.

Unable to resist, Sylvia followed like a sleepwalker. There was an enormous turmoil in her head. It was quite impossible to think. There was the well-scrubbed front step, outlined in white; there was the stone-flagged hallway with the rush matting. It was so important to go inside and find out. . . . Inside to the kitchen.

"Sylvia! Don't go!" The words came from inside her mind. She stopped, unwillingly. She wondered if her mother had heard, too.

"Mmmm . . ." she moaned. She tried harder. "Mummy!" she burst out. "Come back."

She tried to force her legs to go to her mother. She looked down and saw that they were plaid-covered and that she was wearing moccasin-type shoes and thick, knitted stockings.

"I'm coming, Sylvia," said something in her mind.

She made one stumbling step towards Maggie, feeling the strange heavy skirt flapping about her knees. It

Sylvia followed like a sleepwalker.

was like trying to walk in water; she seemed to be making no progress at all. With all her might, she took another step.

And all the while something from the kitchen exerted its incessant, unyielding attraction, as though pulling her towards what had to be done.

Suddenly, frantic and shouting, her father flung himself through the gate, heading for the doorway.

"Sylvia!" he yelled, diving into the hallway and dragging out his bemused wife. "Get into the car, at once!"

Sylvia jerked out of her trance. At the gate she stopped in her headlong dash and looked back at the dirty windows and broken slates. Her legs were once again clad in jeans, her feet in shoes, and the sky was blue and clear.

"What happened, Colin?" asked the dazed Maggie as he helped her into the car. "I don't understand. Why did I have to go into the house?"

"I don't know. Let's just get away from here—right now."

"What made you turn back?"

Colin slipped the key into the ignition. "It was Sylvia. I seemed to hear her cry out, and I felt you both must be in great danger. When I came, Maggie, you were in the hallway." He stared at his wife's sensible jacket and slacks. "And you were wearing a rough plaid dress. . . ."

"With a large brooch," added Sylvia, shuddering uncontrollably. "An old-fashioned, silver brooch with a yellow stone. Oh, please, Dad, let's go away from this place."

Colin put the car in gear. "The two of you must have been caught up in some episode from the past—some tragedy or other. I don't know. But we can't let that happen again. We'll just have to forget the whole business. There's something very peculiar and wrong about that place."

They stopped at the first garage to refuel.

"So, you've been having a look at Mackrin Mains," said the proprietor, unclipping the petrol hose.

"Mackrin Mains?" queried Colin hollowly.

"Yes. Mackrin was the man who built the place—way back in the beginning of the last century," replied the man. "Been renovated several times, but people don't seem to stay there long. Understandable, I suppose."

"Why understandable?"

"Well, because of its history. Some places seem to attract evil—or maybe it's just that they can't rid themselves of the evil that's been perpetrated in them. I don't know. Anyway, it's been empty, off and on, since I was a lad."

"What happened there?" asked Colin, hiding his impatience as, round-eyed and pale, Maggie and Sylvia listened from inside the car.

"Oh, it was too long ago for anybody around here to remember many of the details, but Mackrin was a pig-headed individual, so the tale goes. It was on that spot, he decided, and no other, that he would build his farm house. The word 'mains', by the way, means a farm house."

"Yes," prompted Colin.

"Aye, well, build it he did, and he and his wife and child never knew a happy minute in it. Nobody knows what eventually happened to them. It was said the old ones took them."

"The old ones?"

"Aye, the spirits belonging to the ring cairn," explained the man. "You see, Mackrin built his house on top of a ring cairn. He was told he'd offend the old ones, but as I said, he was a pig-headed man. He even had the effrontery to use the boar stone—that's a carved stone—as part of his kitchen wall."

Sylvia now realised the significance of her dread of the kitchen. Could it have been an old sacrificial place? Her blood chilled, not for the first time that day.

"It's said," continued the garage proprietor, well-satisfied with such an attentive audience, "that the old ones won't be happy until the house has mouldered away completely and there is no stone of it left standing—except the boar stone, of course. Oh, it's been inhabited, but never for long. The old ones make sure of that."

Silently, Maggie and Sylvia watched Colin get back into the car. As though in afterthought, he shouted a question to the garage proprietor. "Can you remember the Mackrins' first names?"

The man was surprised. He scratched his head. "Can't say I ever knew the names of the wife and lassie, but Mackrin himself was baptised Colin. Come to think of it, the tale goes that they disappeared off the face of this earth some time in March over a century ago—the spring equinox, 'tis said." He laughed and nodded. "Aye, and today's March 21st—just as near as you can get to it."

The man waved them off, watching as the car picked up speed on reaching the main road. "Now, why would they want to know the names of the Mackrins?" he wondered.

"Dad, what is a ring cairn?" queried Sylvia.

"Oh, these ring cairns were built around the first or second millenium, before even the Romans came. Some say they had connections with the druids and were places of sacrifice—human sacrifice."

There was silence for some time as the trio came to terms with what had happened. Fright gave way to relief

33

at their escape, and life suddenly became very precious. The sunlight was brighter, the air clearer, and their senses keener with the knowledge that it had so nearly been taken from them.

Sylvia, remembering the rough feel of the long skirt and the clumsy, thong-bound moccasins, ran a grateful hand down her trousered legs. Trembling, she reached out and touched the material of her mother's jacket. Just to make sure, she leaned forward to check that it wasn't home-spun, dark green plaid, held together at the neck with a heavy yellow-stoned brooch.

Sensing the reason for her daughter's gesture, Maggie caught her hand and shuddered in remembrance. "If Sylvia had gone into the house . . . on such a day as this . . . a sacrificial day . . ."

"But she didn't! The chain of events was broken when I sensed her fear and she tried to get to you to stop you," said Colin Mackrin hoarsely. He was silent for some minutes. "If other people couldn't find happiness in that house, what chance would we have had, with a name like Mackrin?"

THE GHOST WITH A LONG MEMORY

by Pat Klacar

WE had grown used to our ghost over the years, so much so that we hardly ever mentioned her to outsiders unless the subject of ghosts happened to come up, and then most people thought we were joking. We never bothered to insist—it didn't matter to us whether other people believed in her or not. As far as we were concerned, she was *there*—every evening, curled up in the big armchair by the drawing-room fireplace, winter and summer, minding her own business, thinking her own thoughts.

I don't know where she went in the daytime, but when the grandfather clock struck six, whoever was using her favourite chair would vacate it without delay. Not that Serena made a fuss if some unsuspecting visitor chose to sit there, she would merely remove herself to wherever it was she went to when she was not with us; but she was such a good judge of character that the guest was rarely invited to our house again!

It was only someone Serena didn't like who couldn't see her. Newcomers she approved of turned into firm friends of ours and accepted her as another member of the family. I don't remember anyone being in the least afraid of our ghost.

Until Mr. Ibbotson came.

Dad hadn't liked him when they met and we didn't expect Serena to let herself be seen, so we were all surprised when he stopped dead in the doorway, his face paling.

"I didn't think to ask whether you had a cat," he said. "I'm allergic to them."

"Oh, don't worry, Mr. Ibbotson," said my mother, "she's not a real cat."

He blinked. "But it moved," he objected. "Don't tell me it's *clockwork*!"

"Certainly not," explained my sister Meg. "And please, Serena is a 'she', not an 'it'."

We knew this from her history. Dad bought the house and a lot of its furnishings after an old lady died, and the niece who was settling her affairs was quite puzzled when someone referred to the cat.

"There's no cat here now," she said. "My aunt did keep one but it pined away and died soon after the funeral."

"A black-and-white cat?" I asked, since she obviously couldn't see the one watching us from the armchair.

"Yes, it was—what makes you ask? Have *you* got one?"

I smiled and shook my head. "Not unless your aunt's decides to stay with us."

"But I told you, it died," said Miss Barlow.

"It must have been happy here," said Meg gently, "because it hasn't gone away."

She leant forward to stroke the cat but her hand passed right through, feeling nothing except a slight chilliness, she told us later. Miss Barlow edged away, looking from the chair to each of us. I tried to look as sane as possible for a nine-year-old boy with a sister only one year younger. (This was three years ago, I'm twelve now and Meg is eleven.)

"A friendly little ghost," Mum reassured Miss Barlow. "What was its name?"

"Serena," she answered, in a faint voice. "It was about eight years old when it——" she gulped—"died."

Dad laughed. "We were planning to find a kitten when we moved to the country. It looks as if Serena has found *us* instead."

Miss Barlow dragged her eyes away from the chair and asked him anxiously, "You're not likely to change your mind about buying the house?"

"Hardly. We like cats and this one won't even want feeding!"

Miss Barlow was in no mood to smile. She couldn't keep her eyes off Serena's chair.

"My aunt used to sit in that chair a lot, the cat on her knee. Supposing she, too——?" Miss Barlow found it difficult to say any more.

"Was she a frightening kind of person?" asked Dad.

"Indeed no," Miss Barlow was emphatic. "But if she's a *ghost*——!"

"She's not here now, Miss Barlow," I said, "so I don't think we need worry."

I was right—we never had any cause for concern. Not until Mr. Ibbotson came, three years later.

Dad had met him through his business, so although he wasn't very nice, when he started hinting he would like a country weekend Dad felt we had to invite him. He looked as if he needed the air, all flabby and unhealthy-looking as he was, but I wondered how he'd stand up to a good long ramble with Roger. Roger was the labrador we bought in order not to offend Serena with another cat—Roger won't go near the drawing-room, but that's just because dogs can't stand ghosts, not because Serena tried to frighten him.

The only person Serena ever frightened was Mr. Ibbotson. He stayed put in the doorway, staring at her, and Serena stared back. We'd never seen her look like that, her eyes blazing and her tail twitching. She seemed to grow as we watched.

"Serena, did you say?" whispered Mr. Ibbotson.

Nobody answered, we were all struck dumb.

"What's the matter, Serena?" I croaked at last.

She turned her head to glance at me, a polite gesture to show she'd heard, but then her fiery eyes turned back to the man rooted in the doorway.

"We'll go into the dining-room," said Mum, making an effort. She almost pushed Mr. Ibbotson outside into the passage while the rest of us followed.

I turned back and Serena was still bristling. I shivered, glad I wasn't the object of her displeasure.

"I'm sorry, old chap, we've never known her behave like this before," Dad apologized.

Mr. Ibbotson sank into the nearest chair, looking sick.

"Why didn't you warn me?" he muttered.

"Not everyone sees her, only those who *like* cats and

don't mind a ghostly one," explained Mum. "We don't like to upset people who won't even know she's there."

"But it's *evil*," shuddered Mr. Ibbotson.

"She's not!" cried Meg. "Serena wouldn't harm anybody—well, not unless they deserved it."

"Meg!" warned Mother, but our guest was not listening.

"Serena," he said to himself, as if he couldn't believe in the name. I didn't blame him—she was anything but her usual serene self.

Meg and I made our escape and went back to the sitting-room, but Serena's chair was empty.

"He must be pretty awful, Rob, for Serena to behave like that," said Meg.

"Perhaps he's one of those people who turn cats into fur gloves," I suggested, but my sister seemed to think I was joking and only scowled at me.

"I wish you could tell us what's wrong, Serena," she said in the direction of the chair.

"I can't make out why she let him see her if she didn't like him," I mused. "Unless she wanted to frighten him away from here for some reason."

We continued to look at the chair but Serena wasn't going to be helpful. And Mr. Ibbotson was not frightened away.

In fact, by the time we'd finished dinner that evening he was quite cheerful, for him, and it was warm enough to invite him out to the garden afterwards so he didn't need to be reminded of his fright in the drawing-room.

It was dark when I woke up. I usually sleep like a log once I'm in bed and I couldn't make out what I was doing awake now in a silent, dark house.

Suddenly, a weird, wailing noise broke the stillness of the night and the hair prickled on my neck. The sound lingered, then died away slowly. I lay rigid, watching my door which was opening slowly. I could make out the pale blur of a figure——

"Rob, are you awake?"

It was Meg, shielding the faint glow from the torch she always keeps by her bed in case the electricity fails. I sat up abruptly and switched on my lamp but hastily switched off again when she hissed, "Put it out!"

"What is it?" I whispered.

"Listen!"

The wail came again, warbling slightly, and this time it was joined by another, in a different key.

"Cats," I said in disgust, ashamed of myself for not thinking of them at first.

A third voice joined in, high and sweet, to be followed by a throaty howl. More and more cats—the whole countryside had gathered to sing in our garden! It might have seemed funny but it wasn't. It was eerie.

"I've never heard them before," said Meg in a scared voice. "I've never even seen a cat within a mile of here. I thought Serena kept them away."

Meg is a light sleeper. She never misses anything in the night, however soundly the rest of us sleep through thunderstorms or anything else.

"Where's Roger?" she asked.

Roger was not in his usual place, the basket by my door. Roger was under my bed, shivering and resisting all our efforts to coax him out.

"Oh come on, boy, don't be daft," I urged him. "Wouldn't you like to go and chase those noisy cats away?"

No, he wouldn't.

I slipped out of bed and found some plimsolls.

"I'd better go and get rid of them before they wake Mum and Dad——"

"Oh! And Mr. Ibbotson!" exclaimed Meg, clapping her

free hand over her mouth while the torch waggled in her other hand.

There was no moon and I couldn't see a thing in the garden. All was still, not a sound. I hissed and slapped at the bushes but there was no frantic rustling of fleeing felines, wherever they had been they had gone now and we heard them no more that night.

At breakfast Mr. Ibbotson declared he had "not slept a wink" thanks to the cats.

"Cats?" repeated my father. "We never get any cats round here. Sure you weren't dreaming, Harry?"

"I was wide awake," said Mr. Ibbotson, grimly.

"I didn't hear anything," said Meg. "I was awake in the night, too."

I stared at her, startled by such an outrageous lie, and she rested one hand on the table, the first two fingers casually crossed. Mr. Ibbotson glared and Mother hastily passed him the butter dish.

"What was *that* for?" I asked Meg as soon as we could get away.

"I just had a feeling," she answered slowly. "I think Serena must have had something to do with bringing all those cats, don't you?"

It was Saturday and Mr. Ibbotson was taken by Dad for that long ramble with Roger, which I don't think any of them enjoyed. After lunch, we went to a garden fête at the vicarage and for once it stayed fine, so we were almost the last to leave, Meg and I carrying prizes and the home-made cakes and jams that poor old Mum feels she has to buy at these events. Mr. Ibbotson had gallantly bought her some flowers, although our own garden is full of them and she'd already used up all the vases in the house.

After we'd washed and changed we all wandered into the drawing-room as usual, quite forgetting about Mr. Ibbotson until suddenly our eyes were drawn to Serena's chair.

She had been lazily washing but now she was standing up, back arched and every hair bristling, almost giving out sparks. With one accord our eyes swung to the door, where our guest hovered, unable to come any further but equally unable to back away.

"Oh, Serena, do behave," said Dad.

Then Serena did something that we'd never seen her do before: she jumped off the chair. More than that, she took a flying leap across the room in the direction of Mr. Ibbotson, who flung up his hands in horror to ward off a spitting, clawing fury.

Only, before she reached him, Serena disappeared.

Outside the window we heard the first gentle, eerie wail, followed by a scrabble of paws as Roger rushed in from the garden, straight through the kitchen and up the stairs to my bedroom!

Dad leant out of the window but the cats started calling from the other side of the house. And then they were joined by other voices further away—nearer—from the orchard—from every direction. We were surrounded, besieged by cats!

We stood transfixed, staring at one another, until at last Mr. Ibbotson tore himself away and fled upstairs.

"Please stop, Serena," begged Meg. "He's only here until tomorrow."

The silence that followed was nearly as frightening as the noise that had gone before, and then Serena was back in her chair, licking a paw as if nothing had happened.

"You saucy thing, you," I said.

She winked at me as the paw swept over one ear, but then she paused in mid-lick as if caught by a sudden thought, her eyes gazing levelly into infinity. I shivered. If I understood Serena's expression as I thought I did, Mr. Ibbotson had more trouble to come.

I thought he would want to leave but he said he was too

ill, so Mother took him some dinner in his room and we were able to enjoy ours. We didn't have to be polite and miss our favourite television programmes, either, and we were all together in the sitting-room when we heard a terrible uproar overhead, things falling about and Mr. Ibbotson shouting. Without really thinking about it, I glanced at Serena's chair. She wasn't in it.

We raced upstairs, Meg and I in the lead with Dad close behind.

The commotion was coming from my bedroom!

The sight that met our eyes halted us in the doorway. We just couldn't believe it.

Mr. Ibbotson was rolling about on the carpet, his eyes tightly screwed shut, flailing his arms as if he were fighting off some demon that was attacking him—only there was nobody else in the room.

"Take them away!" he screamed. "Get them off me!"

"Who? What?" cried Dad, trying to drag the demented man to his feet.

"Has he gone mad?" Mother had caught up with us and was gazing at her unwelcome guest in horror.

"They're clawing me to death!" screeched Mr. Ibbotson, struggling in Dad's arms.

"There's no-one here but us," said Dad, shouting in an effort to get through.

Mr. Ibbotson went limp and opened his eyes, looking around dazedly.

"Where have they gone? There were cats everywhere," he whispered. "They all came at me at once——"

"But what were you doing in here?" asked Mum, bewildered.

"Something fishy," I said, going over to kneel by the hole in the floor that Mr. Ibbotson had opened up.

He had pulled out my bed and rolled back the carpet from that corner, then prised up some of the floorboards. I fumbled inside, hoping I wouldn't touch anything creepy, and brought out a cheap tin cash-box. It wasn't locked, and inside——

"Whew!"

Dad whistled and the rest of us just gaped. I don't think we'd ever seen diamonds like these outside a jewellers' shop window, but we never doubted they were real. Even in the shaded light from my bedside lamp they winked and sparkled like living things. Handfuls of them—well, as many as I could hold in my two hands—rings and bracelets and a huge necklace.

"Give them to me, boy!" snapped Mr. Ibbotson, shaking my father off and darting towards me. He dug one hand into my shoulder so that I cried out, and grabbed the diamonds.

It all happened so quickly that none of us had time to move and Mr. Ibbotson was able to dive past Meg and my mother, knocking them aside as he ran for the stairs. But there he made a big mistake, for the next moment he gave an awful scream and went tumbling. He managed to save himself from going right to the bottom, but he was half way down, twisted up and groaning, clutching his shoulder and one ankle. The diamonds lay all around him in a glittering heap.

As I looked down, I thought I caught sight of Serena slinking through the door to the drawing-room, tail jauntily erect.

Mr. Ibbotson snarled like a trapped cat himself but there was nothing he could do to stop us calling the doctor and the police. He was never a very good criminal, I'm afraid.

We discovered that he was the nephew of the old lady who used to live in our house, and when he came to stay he used to have my room, so when he burgled someone's house he hid the jewels there. The silly man had been caught the next time he tried to break into a house and the police had his fingerprints on file from the other robbery, so he was in prison when his aunt died. When he was released, he tried to find some way of recovering the jewels he had hidden in my room, but, of course, we were always in the house, so he had to pretend to know something about Dad's business and then wangle an invitation.

Mr. Ibbotson got quite a shock when he first walked in and saw Serena. Miss Barlow, the old lady's niece, told us the cat had always hated him and his aunt had always wondered why Serena would growl as soon as she saw Mr. Ibbotson, scratching him if she got the chance. As I said before, Serena was a good judge of character.

Was? Yes, after that Serena left us. I suppose she felt she had done her good deed on Earth, having waited for Mr. Ibbotson to come back. We still miss her, but it's funny—when the police had taken Mr. Ibbotson away and the house was quiet again, we found a black-and-white cat curled up in Serena's chair. A real, live cat who purred and let us stroke her—insists upon our stroking her, whatever else we may be doing at the time! I think she must be a great-great-great-granddaughter of Serena. She's just as wise and very choosy about our friends, but she's livelier—well, she's alive. We call her Allegra, which is the nearest we could get to the opposite of Serena. Roger is quite friendly with her, but he still refuses to enter the drawing-room—maybe Serena's ghost has left a ghost?

COBWEBS

by Terry Gisbourne

"Now, watch this."

Sammy picked a tiny piece of black fluff from a pocket of his blazer and rolled it into a ball. Then, very carefully, he lodged it on one of the fine strands of cobweb and stood back.

"Shhh," he whispered, putting an index finger over his lips.

Suddenly, a black speck appeared from under a ledge of dusty brickwork and settled on the fringe of the web. After a pause it moved furtively forwards just a fraction and stopped. A spider, the hungry keeper of that delicately spun trap, was ready to strike. His front legs lightly fingered the taut threads of glistening gossamer. Then off he sprinted as fast as his eight legs could carry him, down and across the web in pursuit of his "prey". A second more and he would have been on top of it, but the canny spider stopped dead in his tracks and scuttled back to his lair.

Sammy smiled.

"He won't be fooled again by that little trick. You wouldn't think it, but spiders are very clever things."

Sammy's sister, Rebecca, wasn't looking. She had covered her face with her hands.

"What's the matter? You're not afraid of them, are you?"

Rebecca shook her head.

"I can't stand cobwebs. Just the thought of one clinging to my face makes me shiver."

"Girls," grunted Sammy in disgust. "You're all the same."

The sound of approaching footsteps made them look round. It was Mr. Thacker, the history teacher, and he didn't look in a very good mood.

"So that's where you are. Do you realise I've spent nearly half an hour searching for you?"

Mr. Thacker was tall, balding and beady-eyed, with menacing bushy eyebrows and a dark moustache that bristled as fiercely as his temper. He was a daunting sight in or out of the classroom.

It wasn't wise to get on the wrong side of "Old Thack". His deadly aim with the blackboard chalk, and even the rubber itself, was notorious.

Sammy and Rebecca wore guilty looks as they listened to his stern lecture.

"What a fine pair you are! The school gives you a day out to visit one of the finest examples of a mediaeval castle, and what do you do but idle the time away playing games on the battlements. It's just not good enough."

"But sir," Sammy protested, "I was just showing Rebecca how a spider gets its food."

Mr. Thacker looked towards the heavens and sighed.

"That's all very well, lad, but this is supposed to be a practical history lesson, not natural history. Or perhaps you didn't know. Anyway, come on both of you before I lose my temper. We've got to find the rest of the school party now. They should just about be entering the Great Hall."

Rebecca pleaded with Mr. Thacker.

"Please don't be cross, sir. We didn't mean to wander off."

Mr. Thacker's severe gaze relaxed. He even managed to smile a little as Rebecca looked up, her pretty brown eyes expressing deep concern. That dainty face with the up-turned nose and dark curly hair had won him over.

"Well, perhaps not, Rebecca. You're not to blame. Sammy is two years older than you and at thirteen he should behave a bit more responsibly. Let's forget the whole thing, but remember, I don't want it to happen again."

Sammy and Rebecca Curtis lived in Nettleby Village, Kent, and went to the big comprehensive school at Rochfort, three miles away. Today was a school treat. Their two classes had joined up for a visit to Diplock Castle, a magnificent mediaeval fortress that commanded a sweeping view across the English Channel. Built by Sir Hugo Diplock in 1345, it soared above the cliffs on the Dungeness peninsular.

Sir Hugo, a great soldier and a close friend of Edward III, distinguished himself on the battlefields of Crecy, and played a major part in helping the Black Prince to capture King John at the Battle of Poitiers.

"And here," said the castle guide, "is the only portrait of Sir Hugo."

Sammy, Rebecca and Mr. Thacker had joined the rest of the school party in the Great Hall. The elderly guide was pointing to a full-length contemporary painting of a tall man wearing chain mail armour. He stood majestically carrying his helmet under one arm, and wore a white surcoat with the Diplock coat of arms emblazoned in deep red. Finely-drawn features were framed by receding black hair that hung down to the shoulders.

"Did Sir Hugo die in battle?" asked Sammy, but Mr. Thacker intervened before the guide could reply.

"I'm sure Mr. Milton is anxious to press on with the tour, Sammy. Besides, I can tell you that when we get back to school."

"You're quite right, we must carry on," said Mr. Milton. "But when we've finished seeing everything, I'll tell you the mystery surrounding Sir Hugo, and all about the legend of Diplock."

This created a wave of excitement among the youngsters and they eagerly followed Mr. Milton for a tour of the bedrooms.

As usual, Sammy and Rebecca were the dawdlers. They stopped to look at some of the paintings they had missed earlier, then realised that the rest had already gone up the broad staircase.

"Come on," said Sammy, "we'll really get it now if Thack finds us here."

They hadn't covered more than a dozen paces when Rebecca stopped and turned round.

Sammy began to get irritable.

"What's the matter *now*?"

Rebecca took no notice.

"Didn't you hear a noise just then? It sounded like someone crying."

"Oh, don't be silly. He'll be looking for us."

"But I swear I heard it," Rebecca insisted.

Just then the sound of a low moan and sobbing was quite distinct.

"See, I told you. Now do you believe me?"

Sammy frowned, his eyes searching for the source of the sound. He spotted an open door leading off the hall near the stairs.

"That's the only place it could have come from," he whispered.

The pair of them hurried to the scene, but when they got there the room was in semi-darkness. Sammy plucked up courage and tip-toed inside, stopping in the light of the doorway so that his eyes could get accustomed to the gloom.

There was a wide table near the closed curtains, and

Sammy could just about make out the shape of someone standing nearby with their back to him.

He signalled Rebecca to join him. With her at his side he felt more at ease, though he wouldn't dare tell her that.

He moved towards the still figure.

"Excuse me, but can we help you?"

The dim form raised its head, turned round and moved towards them.

It was a lady. In the half-light they could see she was tall and thin and wore what looked like a long, flowing, purple dress. Her golden hair sparkled as the shaft of light swept through the doorway.

"You answered my call and that is indeed good fortune, little ones," she said gently in a foreign accent.

Sammy gave her a puzzled look. What sort of peculiar talk was this, he wondered.

"I have a surprise for you—a secret. Can you keep a secret?"

"Well, that depends," said Sammy, feeling a little uneasy.

Who was this strange lady? Why did he suddenly feel cold? A prickling sensation at the back of his neck made him shudder. Sammy sensed that danger was at hand. She didn't look as if she had been crying bitterly. Her face was completely composed as if nothing had happened. And those eyes. Could he detect a trace of hardness in them?

"I think we had better go and re-join the others, Rebecca," he said nervously.

Rebecca pulled a face.

"Oh, don't be a spoil-sport. The lady needs our help, doesn't she?"

Just then a great blast of air came from nowhere and blew across the room, banging the door shut. At the same time the room was flooded with light.

"Good grief," gasped Sammy. "I don't believe it."

Rebecca was astonished.

49

"What happened?" was all she could manage to say.

The lady simply smiled.

"Please, don't be frightened."

She looked at Sammy, his face reflecting fear and disbelief.

"Oh yes, I knew what you were thinking, young man. I didn't wish to appear sinister, so I thought a bit more light would set your minds at rest. The dark isn't so comforting, is it?"

"I know what you are," said Sammy accusingly. "You're a ghost—no one could have made magic like that."

She laughed.

"Well, let's just say I'm not an ogre. Ghosts do have their uses and I can assure you I'm very useful."

Rebecca was emphatic.

"I think you're a lovely lady . . . er, I mean ghost."

Sammy didn't comment. Anyway, they were stuck there. Their only possible escape route had been the door, but she had seen to that.

"Now, about that little secret of mine," said the lady. "I think you'll like it because I'm going to make you very, very rich."

"Huh! Even a ghost couldn't do that," sneered Sammy. This annoyed Rebecca.

"Why don't you listen, then perhaps you'll find out."

The lady continued: "In the castle vault are many boxes of gold, and I would like you to have them. If you follow me I will show you."

"I still don't understand," Sammy insisted. "Why us? And why doesn't the owner take the gold?"

"I am the owner and I think you'll agree it's of little use to me now. I chose you because you offered to comfort a lonely, distressed lady, and that in itself deserves a reward."

She then walked over to a huge fireplace and touched one of the lion-shaped sculptures mounted on each side of the open hearth. Sammy and Rebecca heard a rough scraping noise and to their amazement saw that the back wall of the fireplace was sliding slowly back. A dark, enormous cavity was revealed, big enough for a man to get through.

"Just a piece of advice," said the lady. "Keep close to me and you won't come to any harm. The way down is honeycombed with passages and tunnels, and I wouldn't want you to get lost."

She stepped into the fireplace and through the hole, followed by the excited pair.

Once inside, the same piece of magic happened again as light replaced the darkness. They were standing in a long, narrow corridor. The crumbling brickwork was very damp and a sickly, musty smell invaded their nostrils.

But to Rebecca this was nothing compared with the awful things that blocked her way straight ahead—a monstrous, silvery mass of cobwebs. The gleaming strands stretched from one wall to the other.

Rebecca instinctively raised her hands to her face.

"Oh Lord, I can't go through that lot."

The lady held out a reassuring hand.

"Wait, and I'll show you."

A small gust of wind suddenly hovered over their heads, and started to whirl round with terrific force. Then a roar of sound gave way to a howl as the little ball of energy burst and swept forwards, smashing through the web curtain. On and on it went down the corridor until the howl became only a faint echo.

After about thirty yards the corridor veered right and ended abruptly. In its place lay a steep flight of stone steps going down for as far as the eye could see.

Rebecca felt nervous.

"Gosh, it looks an awful long way. Is it very far now?"

"Not far," came the short reply.

51

Sammy and Rebecca exchanged anxious looks.

Ten minutes later the end seemed to be in sight. They approached a stout door with a broad lock and a small iron grille set in the woodwork.

The lady unlocked the door and together they heaved it open. The hinges groaned as if unwilling to give them access. On entering, they found themselves in a small, dusty chamber. It was empty except for twelve big metal caskets standing in one corner.

She produced yet another key and pointed to the collection.

"Now I will show you just how rich you're going to be."

Sammy and Rebecca looked on as she started to unlock every box. They felt the excitement mounting. Then, one by one, she raised back the lids.

The pair couldn't believe their eyes. It was a fantastic sight. Cases packed with solid gold bricks, their untarnished brilliance glowing among the grey, sombre surroundings.

They rushed over to examine them. Rebecca tried to lift one and found it a struggle.

"Of course it's heavy," said Sammy. "It wouldn't be gold otherwise." Then he had a sudden thought. "Hey, hold on. How are we going to get them out of here, anyway? There's no other way apart from the stairs, is there?"

Sammy turned round to find the lady.

"Where are you?" he called.

There was a low, wicked laugh and the door creaked as it started to close. Sammy rushed to stop it but he was a second too late. The door banged shut. She had locked them in!

Sammy pushed and shoved and kicked.

"What are you doing? Let us out, let us out!"

The lady's face appeared at the iron grille in the door. Her eyes had an evil gleam.

"This is the penalty you pay for having the treasure. I

kept my promise, but I didn't say you could take it from the vault. You are the new keepers of the fortune, destined to guard over it for ever more. When I think of all the years I've waited for this moment, to be free . . . free . . . free . . ."

Her voice trailed off into the distance.

"Come back!" cried Sammy, banging on the door. "You must be mad. You can't leave us here like this."

Rebecca tried to sound cheerful.

"She's just playing a game. You wait, she'll be back soon. What did she mean by being the keeper of the gold, anyway?"

Sammy looked worried.

"I'm not sure, but one thing is certain—we've been tricked. And if we don't find a way out we're going to rot in here."

First they tried the door again, but it was hopeless. Then Rebecca had a brainwave.

"I know, let's tap the walls. There might be a hollow brick or a secret cavity like the one upstairs."

"Don't be stupid. Haven't you any idea where we are? This vault is right down on the cliff, judging by the steep descent we made."

Sammy banged on one of the walls with his fist.

"It's absolutely solid . . . like you."

"Very funny. And since you're so clever, what do we do now?"

"There's only one thing we can do," said Sammy, giving the walls a final, defeated look. "We'll have to stay by the door and shout and shout until someone hears."

Rebecca frowned at him.

"What's the matter? What are you staring at?"

Suspended two feet above them on the nearest wall was a spider's web.

"Quick, Rebecca," cried Sammy in a burst of excitement. "Help me get one of those boxes over to this wall. First we'll have to take out all the gold, otherwise it will be too heavy to move."

They set about the task as fast as they could, but Rebecca soon began to feel the strain. When finally they came to the last gold bar, she felt as if her arms were going to drop off.

Then they struggled to push the box directly underneath the cobweb.

Sammy stood on top of it and was now able to touch the fine threads. He gave a jubilant cry.

"I was right! There's a stream of air coming through the wall just behind this cobweb. The force of it is making the web move to and fro. That means there must be a cave behind here which comes out of the cliff."

"That's terrific," said Rebecca, beginning to see a slim chance of escape.

"Yes, but just a crack in the wall isn't going to get us out. If there was something like a hammer handy we might be able to knock a hole big enough for us to climb through. It depends how thick the wall is at this point. My guess is that over the years it has gradually eroded and then split, letting in the air. Anyway, we've got to try—it's our only chance."

Their thoughts were interrupted by two faint noises. One, a prolonged booming sound like thunder, was followed by what seemed to be a chuckle. Someone or something laughing!

Sammy looked towards the door, half expecting it to burst open and reveal some monstrous creation that had been spawned centuries ago in the vault.

"Oh Sammy," cried Rebecca, putting a trembling arm round her brother.

Sammy struggled to come to his senses.

"Look, we haven't got a second to lose. We've got to get through that wall somehow."

"What about using one of the gold bars? There isn't anything else."

Sammy didn't stop to argue. In a second he had reached for a gold brick, and resumed his perch on top of the box ready to strike. Using both hands he hit out at the wall. His gold battering ram made quite an impact. Bits of rock began to flake and crumble.

He hit it again and again. There was no doubt about it. The wall was beginning to yield. Small chunks cracked and broke off. Helped by the natural corrosion of the rock, he had soon made a two-inch-deep hole.

Finally, Sammy hit an extra-brittle layer of stone, and nearly lost his weapon as it burst clean through the other side.

"That's great," he gasped. "I didn't think I'd get through as quickly as that."

The weird noises, however, were getting nearer and Sammy's arms felt tired. Dust had caked in the sweat on his face.

Rebecca wanted to take over and get on with the job of widening the hole, but Sammy wouldn't let her. "Anyway, you're too small. You wouldn't reach. Just cross your fingers and hope those noises don't get any louder."

Time seemed to hang heavy as he banged, chipped and hacked away. But in just under two hours the job was done. He had succeeded in making a hole roughly eighteen inches in diameter.

Sammy felt shattered.

"I never want to go through that again," he groaned. "It's amazing what you can do when your life's at stake."

Just then a loud, piercing shriek echoed down the steps outside. Rebecca was petrified.

"Quick, let's go," cried Sammy. "She's coming after us!"

He lifted Rebecca up so that she was within reach of the hole. Then, putting her hands inside, Rebecca started to pull herself through. A few seconds later her head and shoulders emerged on the other side.

"How am I going to get out?" she called. "I can't see the way down. It could be a big drop."

She wriggled forwards and leaned out of the hole, her hands groping for a firm ledge.

"Be careful," Sammy shouted. "I'll hold on to your feet so you won't fall. . . ."

But he was too late. Her legs shot out through the hole before he could grab them. He heard a scream and a crash and then—silence.

"Rebecca! Rebecca! Are you hurt?"

There was no reply. Then Sammy thought he heard the sound of something moving.

"Rebecca, is that you?"

Back came a sharp, impatient, "Yes."

"Are you hurt badly?"

"Not much, no thanks to you," she snapped.

Sammy prepared to clamber into the hole, but suddenly had an uncomfortable feeling that he was being watched. He turned swiftly round and saw the lady glaring at him. She looked very angry.

"Stay where you are," she bellowed.

But Sammy wasn't listening. One look at her and he had scrambled through the opening, and plunged head first into the black emptiness. His left shoulder hit something hard and he toppled over and over, scraping his arms and hands as he went. Thoughts of the falling sensations he used to have in nightmares flashed through his mind. He winced when one of his legs caught a sharp piece of rock.

Eventually, he came to rest, and Sammy found he was lying on his back. Rebecca was standing over him.

"Serves you right," she grinned.

Sammy got up, nursing a few cuts and bruises.

"Well, it could have been worse. Anyway, you seem all right."

"Yes, apart from a badly torn dress and a very sore bottom."

"Come on before she starts to make more trouble for us," said Sammy. "I think there's a light further on."

He began to grope his way along a wall with Rebecca close behind.

The first twenty yards were the most difficult as they stumbled and fell on the slippery stones. But soon it became lighter, with gloomy greys filtering through the darkness. The light was now fifteen yards away, diffusing its rays round a bend in the cave.

Crack!

A sound like the snapping of a swig made Sammy stop and look down. He peered closer.

"Hey, I think I've just stepped on a skeleton."

"Ugh," gasped Rebecca, taking a step back. "Let's get out, quick."

"Silly nit, it won't hurt you. It's probably been here for hundreds of years."

Sammy then noticed that the arms hung from the wall.

"Gosh, that's interesting. The poor bloke must have been left to die here. See how he's been chained to those two metal rings set in the rockface."

Suddenly they heard a rumbling noise, and a small avalanche of stones fell where they had just passed.

"Come on, the place is starting to cave in!" Sammy shouted.

But as Rebecca sprinted towards the exit, she tripped and fell over something round and solid. It was a small wooden cask with metal bands round the sides.

Sammy stopped and urged her to get out quickly. She got

up and made off as fast as she could with the cask under one arm.

The rumbling got louder. A splintering sound became a deafening roar as a mass of rock crashed down only yards behind them. A great cloud of dust billowed in their direction.

They turned the bend and daylight flooded over them. Another two yards and safety. There was the pebble beach at the foot of Diplock cliffs.

Sammy and Rebecca got out just in time. Seconds later the mouth of the cave fell in. Huge chunks of rock now sealed the unknown skeleton's tomb.

Mr. Thacker wasn't very pleased. His bushy eyebrows arched and glowered at the scruffy-looking pair.

"Do you seriously expect me to believe this rubbish about gold in vaults and skeletons?"

But Mr. Milton came to their rescue.

"Well, on the face of it they seem to have some pretty good evidence. We know that a fall of rock has blocked the cave they're talking about. And what about this?"

He picked up the cask that Rebecca had brought with her.

"I'd say that this is definitely a smugglers' cask, and probably contained French brandy. As for your skeleton, it sounds as if he could have been the victim of a smuggling gang. It's a fact that smugglers did sometimes murder accomplices suspected of betraying them."

"But how can you explain the lady and the vault of gold?" asked Sammy.

Mr. Milton laughed.

"I wouldn't like to explain it. You say you have never heard of the Diplock legend. If you had I would have accused you of inventing your story. It's just incredible that it fits the legend as we know it. I don't believe in ghosts, and yet . . ."

"But we would like to know the legend," Rebecca chipped in smartly.

"Well, briefly it goes like this. We know that Sir Hugo was a great soldier, but apparently he was also a very greedy one. He once vowed to his friends that he would never marry unless the lady of his choice had enough gold for it to take ten of his best horses to get it into the castle.

"Shortly after this he went abroad and returned a year or so later with a French bride, Isobel de Beaumont, and a gold fortune that even Sir Hugo had never imagined. It took twelve horses to get it home.

"The story then goes that he and Lady Isobel often quarrelled. She had hidden her riches away where he couldn't find them.

"One day Sir Hugo left the castle and never came back. For a year Lady Isobel roamed the castle, weeping bitterly for his return. Then, with her servants, she set off to find him. She was never seen again.

"They say that the lady haunts the castle still weeping and hoping she can persuade someone to take the gold. That, according to the legend, is the only way her spirit can be free."

"Phew," said Sammy. "All I can say is she very nearly succeeded."

Rebecca sighed.

"But it's an awfully sad story."

A week later the castle trust gave permission for experts to examine the huge fireplace where Sammy and Rebecca said they had entered the corridor leading to the vault. They spent two days probing for the hidden recess, but without success.

The weeping lady still haunts the castle.

Rebecca, however, has one small thing to thank her for. She has never since been afraid of cobwebs.

SPLENDID ANCESTOR

by Mary Clarke

ROSEMARY HART lay in bed and looked at the portrait hanging over the mantelpiece. For years it had laid among the things in her gran's attic and she had never seen it until that morning.

Now Gran was dead, and the portrait was one of the things inherited by Rosemary's mother.

"It's a picture of your great-great-grandfather," Mrs. Hart told Rosemary. "Would you like it for your own? You can hang it in your room."

"Gosh! Yes please," Rosie said. "That would be super. He's marvellous. Sort of . . . royal." She looked at her mother critically. "A bit like you, too, in a way."

Mrs. Hart laughed and patted her shoulder.

"I don't think there's anything royal but he was my great-grandfather so there could be a family likeness. I wouldn't mind being like him in character. He was very brave. Quite a hero in Queen Victoria's time."

"Was he a soldier?" Rosie asked eagerly. History was one of her favourite school subjects, and when she read of happenings of days gone by she used to think of herself as one of the people involved. Perhaps a queen or a lady-in-waiting.

"Great-Grandpa died in the Crimean War," her mother told her. "Even though he was badly wounded, he rallied his troops at the Battle of Inkerman and led them against the Russians. He never thought of his own

60

safety. He kept on fighting until he fell off his horse, dying. It was said that his action played a decisive part in winning the battle."

During the day, Rosie thought a lot about her ancestor. She chose a title to go with his name because, she thought, you can't keep on saying Great-Great-Grandfather Gregory. It was too long even to say in your head. And, in her head, she found she had a great deal to say to him. Or at least to his picture hanging up there on the wall.

So she called him Guardian Gregory, and sometimes just Gregory because he seemed so real to her—like a best friend. He made her feel secure, as she used to feel when she was much smaller, when her father was still with them and she had slipped her hand into his to cross a busy road.

Now tonight, lying in bed, she felt warm and cosy. Quite different from before. She always used to have a frightened feeling about turning out the light and being left in the dark. She had never told her mother about it because it seemed silly to admit to being scared of the dark at ten years old. It was different from thunder and lightning which even her mother didn't like.

But now she had Gregory watching over her and that made it all seem very different. If he could lead soldiers in battle, he could certainly take care of a girl who was his relation. And, with such an ancestor, she just htd to be brave. She couldn't let him be ashamed of her.

After a while, she resolutely pushed back the bedclothes, got out of bed, stole across to the windows, and drew back the curtains. She had never, never, done such a thing before. She had always kept them shut tight because moonbeams stealing in had a nasty way of turning into vampire shapes on the walls.

She turned from the windows and looked up at the portrait. Gregory's eyes followed her back to bed. Jumping in, she smiled at him and saw his approving glance.

"Goodnight, Gregory," she said. Without the slightest hesitation, she put out her hand, switched off the light, and snuggled down into bed.

She had only been asleep a short time when she saw Gregory get down out of the picture frame, mount his horse, jump it through the window, and gallop across the garden.

"Don't leave me, Gregory," she cried. "Don't leave me, *please*."

"I've got to defend you from the invaders!" he shouted back over his shoulder. Rosie crouched there, watching. Her mouth was dry with terror and her heart thumped as she saw a multitude of enemy soldiers advance.

She saw her ancestor rally his small band of men, saw him raise his great sword, heard him cry "charge", and witnessed him hurl himself into the advancing horde. Then he was struck down, but not before the tide of battle had been turned.

She went to him as he lay dying. "Rosemary, be brave. There is nothing to fear," she heard him say. She knelt beside him, weeping and holding his hand until he died.

Then she folded his hands on his chest and put in them a big bunch of red flowers she picked from the battle-field.

In a moment the flowers took root and sprang into gigantic plants. Great thorns grew out of them like octopus tentacles and snaked out towards the enemy horde, driving them still further back. The thorns tangled into grotesque shapes and formed a hedge so strong and dense that it made a barrier between the enemy and Rosie kneeling beside Gregory.

A few of the enemy picked up swords and hacked at the hedge. Some got through. Rosie ran as fast as she could to get away from them but her feet were dead weights. Again and again she tripped over on the bumpy ground. An enemy soldier stretched out his hand to grab her. With a mighty effort she got up and leapt across a river just as a lasso was curling round her feet. She fell flat on her face in the soft mud of the river bank.

Suffocating, gasping for breath, she woke up with her face buried in her soft pillow. Her pyjamas were damp with sweat and the bedclothes were a tangled mess around her legs.

For a moment she lay still, afraid that a hand might grab her or that the great thorny hedge was closing round her bed. But everything was quiet. She was in her own room. The battle had all been a terrible dream.

Then a ghastly thought came to her mind. Had the portrait of Gregory been a dream too? Perhaps she hadn't after all got a wonderful ancestor to help her to be brave.

By the light from the windows she could see something hanging over the mantelpiece. But it might only be the old picture of cows in a meadow which had never meant anything special to her. She had got to find out whether her guardian was still there watching over her.

Cautiously she put out her hand and, keeping her eyes shut, switched on the bedside lamp. She was a bit afraid

An enemy soldier stretched out his hand . . .

that instead of Gregory there might be a Russian soldier over there by the wall.

She opened her eyes a slit and looked through her lashes. In the light of the lamp, she saw Gregory looking down at her, calm and kind.

She sighed happily. "You're still there. That's good," she said.

"Be brave," she heard him say.

Rosie didn't tell anyone at school about Gregory. He was a secret. The wonderful thing was he went to school with her. She was sure of it. If not, she couldn't have played that ghastly game. She had always hated it.

They had to make a circle. One girl stood in the middle and swung a rope round, weighted at the end with a heavy pad. When it came near, you had to jump so that the rope passed under your feet. She was always afraid of jumping too soon or too late. If too late, the rope hurt your legs. If too soon, you messed up the game anyway. Then Miss Briggs, the P.T. teacher, made sarcastic remarks and the other girls laughed.

Rosie tried to get over making mistakes by jogging about all the time so that she was ready to leap at the right moment. Miss Briggs soon stopped that. She said the whole point of the game was to test and quicken reactions. So she pretended to have pains in her legs so that she'd be excused. Even her best friend called her a coward over that.

But now, with Gregory, everything was different. Miss Briggs praised her: "You really are improving," she said. Of course, the teacher didn't know that Gregory was whispering, telling her to keep calm. Then he said: "Now! Jump!"

Rosie felt she simply had to find out more about

C

Gregory. She went to the adult library and asked to borrow a book on the Crimean War.

"That's difficult reading at your age," the librarian said. "Are you sure it's what you want?"

Rosie nodded. "Yes, it is." The librarian was nice, so she added: "Because my guar . . . because someone in our family fought in the war and I've got a portrait of him. I want to find out more about the battles."

Sitting in the playground at lunch time she read the history of the Battle of Inkerman, and shuddered at the sufferings of those involved. Poor soldiers, she thought. She pictured Florence Nightingale going among them, nursing them as best she could. Had Gregory ever met Florence, she wondered?

Perhaps she would be a nurse when she grew up. She saw herself walking through a ward smiling to all the sick people in the beds and they were smiling back. Then she saw herself all in white, going down the church aisle to where a tall soldier, with his hand on the hilt of his ceremonial sword, stood waiting for her.

"Bookworm!" a girl in the playground shouted, and Rosie bounced back to the present. She turned a page of her book and there was his name! Her ancestor was in a history book! Captain Gregory Hassocks. She dwelt on the wonder of it. In her mind, she saw a quiz on television. The question-master asked: "Who was Captain Gregory Hassocks?"

Everyone pressed their buzzers, and the first one said: "He was the hero of the Battle of Inkerman."

She was so proud she could have burst. No one is going to call me a coward again, she vowed. I'd be ashamed to let Captain Hassocks down.

She was longing to show her mother the book and, when she went home, she ran from the bus stop. But her

66

mother wasn't at the door watching for her like she usually was. Rosie had to ring and wait. As she waited she started to feel afraid. Suppose her mother had been knocked down in the street! Or suppose she had been taken ill!

The door was opened quite suddenly by a big, ugly, evil-looking man.

"So . . . you're back home from school, my dear," he said.

He stepped back to let her by, and she saw her mother, pale and shaky, standing uncertainly behind him.

"Oh, Rosie, my darling." she said, almost crying. And then, to the man: "Now will you please go! I've told you—we don't need any work done. So, please—just leave us alone."

"Rosie," the man said. "That's a pretty name." His drawling voice terrified her. "Pretty kid, too." He turned to Mrs. Hart. "You wouldn't want anything to happen to her, would you? Like a nice scar on that pretty face." The drawl became a snarl. "Would you?"

In Rosie's ear, another voice, a very different voice, whispered, "Be brave." And in her heart she answered, "I will, Gregory. I will."

Aloud, she heard herself say to the man, "If you don't go at once, I'll phone for the police."

"Spirit, eh?" the man laughed. "I've taken care of that, my girl. The wire is cut." He spread out his hands. "Look, my dears, it's simple. I'll come clean. I don't want to mend your roof or do any work. Not really. I'm on the run and I need some money. Give me all you've got and twenty-four hours to get clear and I'll be off. No one hurt and all good friends."

Rosie stood up straight and faced him. "You're soppy," she said. "People don't keep money in the house

67

nowadays—not enough to be of any use to you, anyway. They use cheques."

He made a face at Mrs. Hart. "Bright girl, isn't she?"

Rosie looked at her mother. She sat in a chair, white and utterly exhausted.

"Don't worry, Mummy," she said calmly. "Daddy will be home any minute now."

The man laughed aloud. "You're a trier, Rosie, my girl. I happen to know your dad's been dead for years. I do my homework too, you know. I made a few enquiries before I came here. It's marvellous what you can get out of neighbours and shopkeepers by asking the right questions."

His manner changed abruptly and he leapt to his feet. "Come on," he said gruffly. "Let's have a bit of action around here."

He strode over and stood behind Mrs. Hart, putting his hands round her throat. Rosie stood there, her fists clenched. She must stop him. But how? How?

"I'll do her, then you, you cocky little whipper-snapper," the man snarled, his hands tightening on Mrs. Hart's throat.

"Gregory, Gregory, stop him!" Rosie screamed hysterically.

The man looked startled and dropped his hands.

"What's going on," he demanded. "Who's this here Gregory?"

Rosie saw Gregory first. He was standing beside her mother's chair. He was in his captain's uniform and he held aloft his great sword from the Battle of Inkerman —the sword he had thrust through many an enemy. Rosie had no doubt at all of what she saw, but did her mother and the man see him too?

Mrs. Hart shivered. "It's cold," she said, and Rosie

knew that she had felt his presence. But the man? Was it only her scream that froze him?

Suddenly the whole of the man's body quivered. He clenched his fists and swallowed hard, trying to get a grip on himself. He swayed and sank into a chair.

"Oh, my God, my heart," he breathed. "After all these years."

His face and body contorted and he groaned piteously, pressing a hand to his heart.

"Help me, help me," he cried. "It's like a knife being pushed into me." He straightened up to relieve the agony, then fell to the floor.

Much later, when the excitement had died down and the police and ambulance had gone, Rosie went upstairs. She stood in front of the portrait.

"Oh Gregory, you were so wonderful. Thank you very much," she said and burst into tears. Gregory looked down and smiled tenderly. Rosie dried her eyes and smiled back.

She was sure he mouthed, "We managed it between us, didn't we?"

And then—or was it the curtain moving against the moonlight? No, Rosie was certain. The portrait quite definitely winked at her.

ISOBEL'S PONY

by Christine Pullein-Thompson

"You do remember the children, don't you?" asked Mummy on our way to the station. "We all met at the British Museum when you were quite small. Clara bought you a packet of fudge."

I nodded. Clara was Mummy's cousin.

"Shall I call her Aunt Clara?" I asked. There was a knot in my stomach. I hated leaving home, but, most of all, I hated leaving my dun pony, Crispin.

"Yes, and call George, Uncle George. It sounds more polite. I expect Clara will meet you at Meadowhill. And *remember*—don't talk to strange men on the train."

We had reached the station. Mummy had made me wear a skirt, which I had topped by my favourite sweater which was orange with a polo neck.

My train was waiting. "Have a good time," said Mummy, kissing me goodbye. "And don't worry. Uncle George and Aunt Clara are very kind."

"Say goodbye to Crispin for me," I answered, though I had said goodbye to him three times already. "I hope he will be all right. I hope Mr. Chambers will remember to check his water. I hope he doesn't get laminitis. I hope . . ."

But now the train was pulling out of the station and Mummy was getting smaller and smaller, until at last I could see her no longer.

I shut the window and tried to read a book, but I couldn't concentrate. I had never been away on my own before and I kept wondering what would happen if Aunt Clara and I failed to recognize each other. Or if I alighted at the wrong station. Or if I hated her children. Or, worse still, they hated me.

Meadowhill station was small and bathed in sunlight when I reached it, I could not see Aunt Clara anywhere. I stood on the platform trying to keep calm, holding my small suitcase. The ticket collector eyed me anxiously. A puppy, nailed down in a crate, whined. Outside, birds sang.

"There she is!" shouted a voice, and two boys dashed into the station while behind them a girl called, "Wait, don't we need platform tickets?"

70

They had long hair and wore jeans and tee shirts.

"Isobel Browne?" said the eldest. "Here, let me take your case."

The girl was dressed in the same way, but her hair was longer still.

"I was looking for Aunt Clara," I said.

"Well, we'd better introduce ourselves," said the largest boy. "I'm Larry. This is Paul, and this odd-looking female is called Patricia."

"Shut up, beast," replied Patricia, aiming a kick at him.

I remembered them as small in fitted coats and with short, brushed hair. In those days they had had a nanny. They had been meek and polite, wearing patent leather shoes and white ankle socks.

"Sorry about the old bus," said Larry now, opening the door of a battered car. "The old man won't subscribe to anything better."

"Larry gets through a car a month," said Paul.

"Did you have a good journey?" asked Patricia.

"Yes, thank you." I felt small and out of place, and idiotic in my skirt.

Their house looked across a small, tumbling river to wooded hills. Beside it stood the remains of a castle.

I looked hopefully in the fields for ponies, but there were none. Larry parked the car in front of the house and kicked off his shoes.

"Patricia will show you your room," he said, throwing my case at his sister.

She caught it and, saying "Beast!" again, led me barefoot up a wide flight of stairs. "He's mad," she said. "It's very sad. Where have your parents gone?"

"Rumania and Hungary. Daddy's selling agricultural machinery. It's the first time Mummy's gone with him," I replied.

"Lucky them."

71

My bedroom window looked across the remains of the castle to the tree-shadowed river. Once the castle must have dominated that particular stretch of the river completely; now only some of its outer walls remained, while, inside, thistles grew. I imagined knights stepping out of boats, the peaceful splash of oars. Patricia put my case on a chair.

"Did anyone tell you anything abóut this place?" she asked, looking at me anxiously. "I mean, are you nervous? Do you get upset easily?"

"I don't know. I don't think so. It depends. I would be upset if Crispin died, or Mummy, or Daddy."

"Of course," replied Patricia impatiently. "Well, I suppose there's no point in beating about the bush; but I wish Daddy had told you before you came."

"What?" I was beginning to feel alarmed. "About what?"

"About our ghost?"

"What sort of ghost?" I could feel the hair standing up along my back, but when Patricia said, "It's a pony," all my alarm vanished.

"Or it may be a horse, I don't know. It's grey, anyway," she continued.

"Well, I don't mind a horse. I love them. I've got a pony of my own."

"That's all right then," said Patricia, sounding relieved. "The poor animal is looking for something. It only comes at this time of the year and is utterly harmless. See you at dinner; it's in ten minutes. Owly beats a gong." She ran out of the room slamming the door after her.

I sat on my bed, suddenly homesick. Patricia and her brothers have thought up this ghost to frighten me, I thought. What wonderful hospitality! But I'm not going to be frightened, I decided, washing my hands. I'm going to sleep like a top. Wishing that I was as tall and arrogant as my cousins, I put on my oldest pair of jeans. Then a gong boomed and someone called, "Isobel, it's dinner."

Aunt Clara and Uncle George sat at different ends of the large dining-room table. They stood up to shake hands with me. It was all horribly formal. I was made to sit on Uncle George's right because I was a guest. Owly waited at table as she had apparently for the last twenty years. She wore large spectacles—which only partially hid large, owl-like eyes—a black dress and a plain white apron. She called me "Miss Isobel". I used my dessert spoon for my soup and mixed up my knives. Aunt Clara and Uncle George talked to me about agricultural machinery—of which I know nothing. If they had talked about Crispin and the pony club, everything would have been all right; as it was, dinner for me was a small social disaster.

Afterwards Patricia suggested a game of Monopoly and we played until bedtime, sitting at a table in the hall, while Paul sat on the stairs playing his transistor at full volume.

When I retired to bed, I found the curtains drawn and my pyjamas waiting for me on my pillow. The rest of my clothes had been unpacked and put away. I was suddenly very tired. The morning seemed to belong to another life.

Patricia came in to say goodnight. "Don't worry about footsteps in the night," she said. "The boys stay up for hours."

"I won't," I answered, getting into bed.

"Is everything all right?" she asked next, glancing round the room. "Has Owly given you enough towels, soap, everything?"

I nodded. I felt very far from home, and I much preferred my own more humble bedroom with pictures of horses pinned to the walls and my few rosettes above my bed.

"And remember, if you hear a neigh or two in the night,

73

it's just our ghost. Nothing to worry about. A few more weeks and he will be gone until next summer."

"I shall certainly look out if I hear a neigh," I answered. "I've always wanted to see a ghost. But if it's one of your awful brothers pretending, I shall be absolutely furious. In fact I shall throw something at him."

"They're not that mad," replied Patricia, laughing before she left.

I lay in my luxurious bed and, being too tired to read, switched off my elegant bedside light. Moonlight filtered through the curtains, a light wind stirred the trees outside. I could hear Paul's transistor still playing in the distance; otherwise everything was quiet. I wondered whether Crispin had missed my usual evening visit and whether my parents had landed in Bucharest yet. Somewhere in the house a clock chimed ten times. I thought I heard Uncle George saying goodnight to someone. Then a door slammed and there was silence. After that I must have slept, though I cannot remember falling asleep. I know I dreamed that Crispin had escaped from the orchard and that he was neighing. He walked up and down below my window and then he neighed again and this time it was like a call for help. He seemed to be crying, "Come, please come."

And then I was sitting up in bed, sweating, knowing that it wasn't a dream any more, that there really was a pony outside calling to me in the moonlight. My heart started to beat in an idiotic manner. It's the ghost, I thought. Patricia wasn't joking after all. There really is one!

I stepped out of bed on to shaky feet, and a minute must have passed before I found the courage to draw back the curtains and look out.

The moon was partly covered by a cloud, but I could see the pony clearly standing alone in the long grass by the castle. He was looking up, his eyes searching for something or someone. He wore the sort of tack ponies wore long ago, including a saddle which was stained with something that looked like blood. His head was small, set on a fine arched neck, and he shook a long blood-soaked mane before he trotted away like a dancer without looking back.

My teeth were chattering now. I was suddenly certain that I had seen the pony somewhere before. But where? And when? It was obvious he had existed years and years ago; so how could I know him? But the feeling remained and I had difficulty in stopping myself from going down to him. I wanted to put my arms around his poor neck, to comfort him, to say . . . to say what? The words were there, some pet words in the back of my brain, which belonged to him. I'm going mad, I thought. I don't know the pony. I can't. Tears were running down my face now. I opened the window, but the pony had vanished. And now the first of the birds was singing and, above the river, dawn was breaking.

I returned to my bed. So Patricia *wasn't* joking, I decided, putting on the light. There is a ghost. And I know him! Somehow, somewhere, we have met. "But you know that is impossible, Isobel, you fool," I told myself. "He belongs to the days of knights. He's a palfrey. How could you, for pity's sake. Where's your sanity?"

But sanity and reason had nothing to do with it. It was beyond and above such things. I was attracted to him by something far stronger than either, and now my brain seemed to be going round and round in a mad circle, saying, "I want to go to him, I want to go." And I felt as though I was floating across the room and out of the window, as though some great force was dragging me, something I had no hope of withstanding. And then I was crying, "I don't want to go, I don't want to," and Patricia was shaking me and saying, "It's me, Patricia." And I didn't know where the hours had gone, for morning had come and the room was full of sunlight.

"Are you all right?" asked Patricia anxiously, peering into my face. "You look awful."

"As though I've seen a ghost, no doubt," I said, trying to laugh.

"Did you?"

"Yes."

"It's ten o'clock. We couldn't wake you. I've been up here five times."

"He neighed twice," I explained. "I saw him. He's grey."

"That's what he always does. I ignore him now. I think he's a bore, really. But then I'm not crazy about horses," said Patricia, who was looking very healthy this morning. "You weren't frightened, were you?"

"Of course not," I lied bravely, trying to forget the horrors of the night. "I shall be able to tell everyone at school about it. None of them has ever seen a ghost."

"Well, get up then, lazy bones," cried Patricia. "We're going sight-seeing today."

Breakfast was still waiting for me in the dining-room. Aunt Clara was reading a newspaper. She looked up at my approach.

"I hear our ghost came again last night. I hope he didn't worry you. He's quite a friendly ghost really," she said.

"He's super," I answered breezily, helping myself to cornflakes. "What happened to him? Why does he come?"

"It's a long story and rather a sad one," replied Aunt Clara. "I think it might upset you."

"I don't mind," I replied, though I could feel a lump rising in my throat already.

"I'll tell you one day, but not this morning," answered Aunt Clara, returning to her newspaper. "It's too sad for such a lovely day."

76

We looked round the local museum in the morning and, after a cold lunch, Patricia taught me to row on the river. It was one of those golden summer days which, looking back, seem to have had no beginning and no end. I was not very successful at rowing. My restless night had left its mark. My arms felt weak and lifeless and sometimes I felt as though I was a spectator looking at us both from a long way off. It was an eerie sensation. We were too late for tea when we returned to the house, but dinner was formal again, with Owly waiting on us. Aunt Clara stared at me with some consternation as I sat down.

"Are you all right, Isobel?" she asked. "You don't look very well to me. Did our ghost upset you last night? Would you like to have Patricia's room? It's on the other side of the house."

"No thank you. I'm quite all right," I replied quickly, though now Uncle George and Aunt Clara both seemed to be fading into the distance.

"Oh dear, I do hope you're not going to be ill," exclaimed Aunt Clara, growing smaller and smaller every second.

"Give her some water," said Uncle George. "Hurry."

"I'm quite all right," I said, as they came into focus again. "I don't need water. It's just that I keep hearing hoof-beats and someone crying. . . ."

"Oh dear!" said Aunt Clara. "What are we going to do?"

"Nothing. They've gone. I'm quite all right," I answered, spooning soup into my mouth.

The boys had gone out to a party. After dinner, Patricia and I watched television in the small sitting-room by the kitchen which had once been the servants' hall. Aunt Clara popped her head round the door from time to time to ask, "Are you all right, Isobel dear? Quite all right? Are you sure?"

"Yes thank you," I answered each time. "I'm fine."

When we retired to bed, she gave us each a cup of Ovaltine. Mine had two sugar lumps on the saucer and I put them in my dressing-gown pocket.

"Are they for the ghost?" asked Patricia, watching me. "Because he won't eat them. He fades away at the least sound. The boys tried to make friends with him years ago, but he just faded away into the shrubbery with one last, desperate neigh. If you're scared, come into my room. Wake me up. I shan't mind. Promise."

"All right, I promise." I wanted to be alone now, for I felt as though I had an important appointment which I must keep at all costs.

"Goodnight," I said. "Sleep well. See you tomorrow."

I opened my window and leaned out. Everything was still and beautiful; almost too beautiful for the heart to bear. There was hardly a ripple on the river, and the sky was darkening into night. It was easy to imagine the castle as it had been—full of people, with knights coming and going, and a great fire in the hall, horses being led away to stables, the clank of armour. I left the curtains undrawn and climbed into bed, and I must have fallen asleep immediately, for right away I started to dream that I was riding a grey pony. I sat sideways in a long skirt with a groom following on a big horse. Everything was extremely vivid, not blurred nor muddled as dreams so often are. The trees were green with leaves and there were flowers everywhere. I had a feeling of intense happiness, as though suddenly all my dreams were coming true.

I was humming a tune when the neigh rang out, and I sat up in bed instantly, because I had known all along that it would come, that my appointment was with the grey pony outside—whether I wanted it or not. I still wore my dressing-gown and my legs carried me unasked out of the room and down the wide stairs. My hands knew how to draw

78

back the bolts on the door into the garden. The grass was wet with dew and there was a smell of roses which I had not noticed before.

The grey pony stood just where he had the night before, his ears pricked, his eyes searching for me, and now I was running, tripping over the lawn, wrenching open the iron gate. I no longer wore my pyjamas and dressing-gown, but a long skirt which reached to my ankles, a cloak, and a hat with a feather in it.

"Silver!" I cried. "Silver!" And the pony whinnied, recognizing me at once, and all the misery left his eyes. He came towards me as a friend, his nostrils nickering. I held out my hand, with the sugar in it.

I felt his whiskers brush against my fingers, his breath on my hand. Then he gave a loud sigh, a sigh of pure contentment. The sort of sigh one might give when one had reached home after a long and arduous journey. And then, without warning, everything changed; Silver was gone and I was fighting for my life with a cloak over my head. I tried to scream, but no words would come and I knew now without doubt that I was dying, falling into space, into nothingness, and I didn't want to die. And then there was darkness, silent and absolute, and I knew that this was the end. . . .

"He knew me," I said.

I felt as though I had been away for a long time and come back. Mummy was sitting at the end of my bed, wearing her navy blue suit.

"She's coming round!" she exclaimed.

Aunt Clara was sitting in a chair. Sunshine streamed through the cracks in the drawn curtains.

"How did you get here?" I asked, sitting up. "What's the time? Is it Sunday or Monday?"

I held out my hand with the sugar in it . . .

"It's Wednesday, darling," replied Mummy, bending forward to kiss me.

"Give her some water," said Aunt Clara. "Here, take the glass."

"He knew me," I announced again, without really meaning to, rather as a record keeps saying the same thing when the needle is stuck. I drank some water. It had ice in it. "There was blood on his neck. It wasn't a dream, was it?" I asked. "It did really happen, didn't it?"

"Of course, darling," replied Mummy in a soothing voice, the sort of voice one might use to a very small child.

"We found you lying by the castle," added Aunt Clara. "Patricia was anxious, so she went outside to look."

"He was alive because he took the sugar. Is it the same day?" I asked. "The morning after."

"No, you've been delirious for two days," replied Mummy. "I came back to be with you. Don't talk too much."

"I'm so sorry," I answered.

"It wasn't your fault, darling."

"He hasn't been back. I don't think he will ever come back again," said Aunt Clara.

"He knew me. How did he know me?" I asked slowly. "He whinnied to me. He took the sugar." Everything was suddenly crystal clear. "He took the sugar," I repeated. "I know he did. I felt his whiskers."

"Don't get excited," said Mummy.

"We know he took the sugar," Aunt Clara told me. "Patricia searched for it. She looked in your pockets, too."

"Rest, darling," said Mummy. "Lie back. Doctor Perkins will be here again soon."

"I will get you something to eat," said Aunt Clara, tiptoeing from the room.

I felt weak, but happy, too, in a strange, exhausted way. I felt as though I had accomplished something of great importance. Silver's all right now, I thought. He's found peace at last. And I'm going to be all right, too. I'm not even mad and I can move all my limbs and open and shut my eyes and everything works!

Doctor Perkins was tall and dark. He took my pulse and temperature. He looked into my ears and eyes with a torch. He asked me to look in different directions, and knocked my knees with a little hammer.

"We could X-ray her skull," he said, sounding perplexed.

"She seems quite well now—quite her usual self in fact," replied Mummy.

"A spontaneous recovery," said Doctor Perkins. "But keep her quiet for the next twenty-four hours. I will call again tomorrow, unless you're worried."

Aunt Clara showed him out.

"I'm all right," I said. "Why can't I get up? I'm sick of bed. I want to go outside."

"Well, you can't," said Mummy. "Anyway, don't you want to hear the story?"

"What story?"

"Silver's, of course."

"How do you know it?" I was sitting up again now, tense with excitement.

"It belongs to Isobel, too," answered Mummy. "Aunt Clara told me it yesterday when you were delirious. I think the two Isobels were fighting over you, but thank goodness, my Isobel won."

Aunt Clara had returned with a tray covered with cups and saucers and plates, bread and butter, jam, three kinds of cake and a pot of tea with sugar and milk.

"You tell her about Silver, Clara. You will tell it better than me," said Mummy, pouring tea.

"Is she well enough?"

Mummy nodded. "The colour is back in her cheeks. You are feeling all right now, aren't you, Isobel?"

"Yes." I took a piece of cake and waited while downstairs in the hall a clock chimed four times.

Patricia came into the room and sat down on a chair.

"It all happened a long time ago," began Aunt Clara, as though she was reading from a book, and I could see it all in my mind; the ruined castle standing tall and brave with turrets at each end, a landing stage on the river, a flag flying.

"The house wasn't here, of course. Our ancestors lived in the castle—yours as well as ours, Isobel. The castle was big, with dungeons——"

"And turrets at each end," I interrupted.

"Yes. I will show you a drawing of it later."

"And Isobel came on her grey pony, followed by a groom. And there were a great many trees. She came through a forest."

"How did you know?" asked Aunt Clara.

"I just do," I replied.

"She had reared Silver from a foal. They were inseparable," continued Aunt Clara. "She was expecting a baby and her husband had inherited the castle. He was dead, but no one had told her."

"This is the awful part," said Patricia.

"He had died fighting in France. But she was expecting, and, if the baby was a son, he would inherit the castle."

"So she was killed," I cried. "She was happy because she thought she was going to live in the castle with her husband. She thought his relations would welcome her."

"But her uncle-in-law wasn't like that," said Aunt Clara. "He had her brutally murdered when she arrived on a dark September night, and they buried her and her servant where this house now stands."

"He was our great, great, great uncle," said Patricia, biting her nails.

"What about Silver?" I asked.

"They drove him away into the forest, but he kept coming back, so, in a fit of anger, they killed him. But he still came back each September, looking for Isobel."

"Until three nights ago," said Mummy.

"What no one at the castle knew was that Isobel already had a baby girl, your great-great-grandmother," said Aunt Clara.

"I'm sure you haven't said enough greats," exclaimed Patricia.

"And because of your relationship to her, you look like the first Isobel," said Mummy.

"I don't just look," I answered. "I *was* her. I knew I had met Silver before, the moment I saw him. I've just been back through time. But he's all right now. He'll never come back."

Soon after that I fell asleep again, and a day later Mummy and I left to join Daddy in Rumania. I have never returned to the house, but I write to Patricia from time to time, particularly around September, and she assures me that Silver has never been back.

ALICIA

by Louise Francke

SANDERFORD is a yellow cat with yellow eyes and he is never allowed in the attic. But Elizabeth Ann had seen him go up, so she went after him.

She stopped five steps from the top of the stairs. The step that put her eyes just above attic-floor level. She stood quietly for a moment and looked along between boxes and bureau legs for a patch of yellow fur. "Here Sandy, here Sandy," she called softly.

The attic door had been standing open a little. That's strange, she thought. She had seen Sandy's tail disappearing into the darkness, so she knew he was here. "Here Sandy, here Sandy."

He wasn't allowed in the attic. Ever.

"Here Sandy, here Sandy."

"Here, dear. He's over here, dear Alicia," a sweet, soft voice answered. Elizabeth Ann froze. Her mouth dropped open slightly and her eyes grew wide with astonishment as they turned in the direction of the gentle but terrifyingly unexpected voice.

In the chair. In the dainty great-great-grandmother rocker. A pale, pretty, white-haired woman in a delicate blue dress. Right next to the chair sat Sanderford with his tail curled neatly around him. Both of them were looking at her.

"Here, dear." The woman's hand drifted down slowly to touch the top of Sanderford's head. "Here's your kitty. With me. You see? Your kitty is my friend, dear Alicia." She was smiling. But her eyes didn't smile. They seemed hard and brilliant in the dim light.

"My name is not Alicia," said Elizabeth Ann in a faintly choked voice.

"I know. I know, my dear." She spoke softly but quickly. "But you do look like Alicia. You look so very much like Alicia I really don't believe I can call you anything else. You won't mind if I call you Alicia, will you? I have thought of you as Alicia for so long. Ever since I started watching you play in the garden. Right from this window." She motioned towards the small window and her hand looked nearly transparent. "I was hoping you would come. Today. Especially today. Because today you are eleven." Again she smiled sweetly.

Today was, in fact, Elizabeth Ann's eleventh birthday.

"But don't just stand there on the stairway, dear Alicia. Come up, come up." Her voice was soft but urgent. "I've been waiting so long to talk with you."

Elizabeth Ann didn't want to go up. She thought she should go down and tell her mother about this woman sitting in the attic.

"Come," insisted the woman. "Let me show you the picture of my beautiful Alicia. You'll see. You'll see how much you look like her."

"No thank you. Not right now." Elizabeth Ann knew that this woman should *not* be sitting in the great-great-grandmother chair in the attic. "I must go now." Then she remembered why she had come to the attic. "Here Sandy, here Sandy," she called, but Sanderford's tail remained curled around his paws. "Here Sandy, come Sandy." The pale woman had reached into a blue pocket and was holding a small picture out towards her.

"Come and see Alicia first, my dear, and then I will let your Sanderford go with you." What did she mean, *let* him go, wondered Elizabeth Ann. Did she have the power to make him stay there?

No, Elizabeth Ann didn't want to go up. But she put her foot on the fourth step from the top, slowly. Perhaps she would just look at the picture quickly, then take Sandy downstairs. Her foot moved to the third step.

"Yes, yes, come dear. Here it is."

Elizabeth Ann had reached the top and was walking cautiously towards the woman in the chair. Then, with a wave, the picture came fluttering through the air.

As she bent to pick it up from the floor, Sanderford uncurled his tail, walked across the attic and down the stairs.

Elizabeth Ann followed. On the fifth step from the

top she turned her head to look at the woman once more, but the great-great-grandmother chair was empty. Quite empty.

Elizabeth Ann shut the attic door firmly.

Silly, she thought. Silly! Silly imagination. Yes, it is. Yet she had the picture in her hand.

She looked at the pale, reddish-brown portrait. At the small face looking back at her. It's *me*, she thought. It really does look like *me*.

She turned the picture over and read the pencilled inscription: "Alicia Frost, Aged 11." Then she walked into her room and slipped the picture, face down, into her dressing-table drawer.

Elizabeth Ann waited until after dinner. Until she and her mother were alone. She had made her wish, blown out the eleven birthday candles . . . and they had had ice-cream, too.

Now she was drying dishes as her mother washed.

"Who was Alicia, Mother?"

Her mother was slipping more plates into the dishwater and hardly seemed to notice the question. "I don't know, dear. Who was she?"

"I don't know either," answered Elizabeth Ann. "But she was somebody. I found her picture in the attic. On the back it says she's Alicia Frost, aged eleven. That's my age now. And she looks just like me."

"Alicia Frost?" Her mother thought a minute. "Attic? Well, there are some old things in the trunk up there, I think, but I don't remember any pictures. Frost," she repeated. "That was your great-grandmother's name. Yes . . . yes. . . ." She frowned thoughtfully. "Alicia Frost was your great-grandmother's sister. She died when she was a little girl."

87

Elizabeth Ann picked up another plate and rubbed it with the linen towel.

"But . . ." her mother continued, "I don't remember ever seeing a picture of her. Where did you find it? In the trunk?"

"I picked it up off the floor." There, thought Elizabeth Ann. That's the absolute truth. There's no imagination about that.

"Where's the picture now, dear?"

"In my room."

When the dishes were finished, Elizabeth Ann brought the picture down to show her mother. She was almost sorry that she had mentioned it, because now she wanted to tell her mother about the woman in the chair. Yet she knew it would sound foolish. Of course there was no woman in the attic. Even Elizabeth Ann knew that. She had simply imagined it. Hadn't she?

"Yes," said her mother. "That would be your great-grandmother's sister. She must have died right after this picture was taken. It was said that *her* mother—and that would be your great-*great*-grandmother, Elizabeth Ann—went quite mad after her little girl died. And that she wandered around the house for years, searching and calling for her daughter Alicia."

"And that's her chair—my great-great-grandmother's chair—in the attic, isn't it, Mother?"

"Yes, that's right. Just think, it has been in the family all these years."

"Do you think I look like Alicia?"

"Well, I think you do." Elizabeth Ann's mother had put on her glasses and was studying the faded picture.

She handed the picture back to Elizabeth Ann. "Yes, I think you look a lot like Alicia." Then she patted her daughter's hair softly and said, half to herself, "both very pretty girls, very pretty indeed."

The matter was thus dismissed, and Elizabeth Ann didn't really think much about it again until the next afternoon when she was on her way to her room. She heard a faint call. "Alicia-a." She heard it. Distinctly. Definitely. She turned and saw the attic door standing open again.

Elizabeth Ann's heart pounded. I didn't hear it, she commanded herself. I'm imagining it. I won't go. I won't go up again.

"Alicia-a." Faint and soft, but clear.

I won't go. She's not there. She doesn't exist. I'm imagining her. And Elizabeth Ann marched over, shut the attic door, turned her back and went to her room to change her clothes.

She never thought that she might have to pay for her rudeness.

Elizabeth Ann wakened from her sound sleep that night to see Sanderford glowering at her from the foot of the bed, his eyes too bright in the darkness. And behind him stood the woman from the attic, but this time she was not smiling and her eyes were hard and brilliant.

"I called you," she whispered with a tight mouth. "You didn't come. You are a wicked girl. We had been waiting all afternoon and you didn't come."

Her tone frightened Elizabeth Ann and she drew the eiderdown closer to her chin. "You belong in the attic. . . ."

But the woman interrupted, hissing at her, "When I call you, you come. . . ."

Tears of fright welled up in Elizabeth Ann's eyes, her mouth opened to call her mother, but nothing came out.

Abruptly, the expression on the woman's face changed and became both sweet and sad. Sadly sweet.

"Oh my dear, dearest Alicia . . . I didn't mean to frighten you. I missed you, that's all." She was moving, noiselessly, up from the foot of the bed. "Now that we've finally met, you're my own dear Alicia, and I want to see you often. Every single day."

"Go back to the attic," Elizabeth Ann sobbed softly. "Go back to the attic. . . ."

"Of course I will, my dear, dear girl. Of course I will, right now." Her pale hand fluttered up towards Elizabeth Ann's cheek and she touched it softly with what seemed to be real affection. "Just promise, my dear heart, you'll come and see me tomorrow. Come and talk to this lonely old lady."

"I promise,"—though Elizabeth Ann hardly knew she had said it.

Without a sound, the woman drifted quickly toward the door and was gone. Sanderford closed his eyes, curled his paws under him on the bed and was asleep.

The morning was bright when Elizabeth Ann woke with only a vague remnant of an unpleasant dream in the back of her head. She looked at the bottom of the bed where Sanderford was stretching himself awake. He blinked at her and she blinked back, slid out of bed, went to the bathroom and washed her face, looking up into the mirror as she dried it on the soft towel.

There on her right cheek was a small strawberry-red mark about the size of a pea. Elizabeth Ann leaned toward the mirror and rubbed it. The skin was smooth and unbroken. Now what's that, she wondered. And her left-over dream flashed into focus. She stared at the red mark. That's where the woman had touched her. It's a warning. It must be. No! There is no woman . . . no woman at all. She must have dreamed that the woman had touched her the instant some mosquito had pierced her

90

cheek. That's it, she convinced herself. But she rubbed it in doubt on the way down to breakfast.

Mother examined the red mark carefully and agreed with her mosquito theory. "I'll spray your room this morning, so you won't be bitten again tonight."

Elizabeth Ann was preoccupied with her dream all day. As bedtime approached, she became more and more uneasy. Perhaps she should tell her mother. But she knew what the reaction would be—a teasing laugh and a comforting pat with all of the blame given to her lively imagination. No, there was no point in telling anyone.

Bedtime arrived and, for the first time in her life, Elizabeth Ann looked under her bed and into her wardrobe before shutting the bedroom door. And, for the first time in her life, she locked the door, turning the key quietly . . . very quietly. Locking bedroom doors was forbidden. What if someone felt ill in the night and called out?

She propped herself up comfortably with her pillow and turned out the light. I'll just stay awake tonight, she told herself. And she did. For almost an hour.

Then it happened.

Elizabeth Ann was jolted awake by a hard, hurting jerk on her left leg. So hard, it pulled her right off her pillow and her head thumped back on the bed.

Instinctively, she twisted slightly to pull her leg towards her and there, at the end of the bed, was the woman, smiling sweetly, ever so sweetly, with her eyes burning bright in the dark. Both of the woman's hands held Elizabeth Ann's ankle tightly.

Sanderford stood, arched, on the bed, puffed and huge, nearly double his normal size. His mouth was open in a near grin, his eyes furious and glowing.

She heard the hissing whispers . . . "It's time now Alicia-a . . . time to come. You broke your promise to me . . . you promised me . . . you promised to come . . .

but you broke your promise . . . you made me come to get you . . . so I'll take you . . . with me . . . now. . . ."

Elizabeth Ann struggled, but she was being pulled slowly towards the foot of the bed.

"I'll teach you . . . you'll come with me . . . you can't break your promise to me. . . ."

Elizabeth Ann tried to scream, and tried again, but her breath was coming in short gasps as she fought to free her ankle.

"We'll go together now . . . the three of us . . . forever together my dearest, my dearling . . . my own . . . Alicia-a."

Elizabeth Ann pushed, but slipped on the smooth sheet. There was nothing for her hands to grasp. The eiderdown bunched and puffed and turned into soft nothingness in her fingers. She pulled and twisted and hunched her shoulders, but slowly, slowly she was being drawn towards the old woman.

Suddenly, Elizabeth Ann pulled herself upright and grabbed at the hands holding her ankle. She pried at the fingers of one bony hand and felt them weaken, slowly . . . slip . . . let go . . . *her hair*! The woman had seized her hair! One strong hand still held her ankle fast, but the other now gripped her hair and was pulling her head . . . ouch . . . ouch . . . ow-w-w-w. . . . In her pain, Elizabeth Ann clenched both hands into fists and punched out into the middle of the not-so-fragile old woman. She heard a loud *hi-s-s-s-s* of breath as the woman doubled up. The hands let go.

Quickly, Elizabeth Ann rolled off the bed and, as her feet touched the floor, Sanderford's puffed, furry, yellow mass hurled itself toward her, claws digging into her shoulder. Her mouth dropped open and, this time, a piercing scream came out . . . a scream of pain as the cat's claws slid off her shoulder and down her back.

A hand clamped on to her wrist as Sanderford hit the floor with a thud. Elizabeth Ann whirled to face the woman and to pry, again, at the fingers holding her. In the distance there was a pounding on the door, and her mother's voice called, "What's the matter, Elizabeth Ann? What's the matter? Why have you locked the door? ... Elizabeth Ann?"

Her arm was being twisted and she was being pulled now, towards the window. The pounding turned to heavy thuds as Elizabeth Ann shrieked again. The woman's voice was still hissing in her ears, louder now, more cracking. "You'll come ... I have you ... you're mine now, Alicia-a ... you're mine. ..."

An agonizing twist of her arm and Elizabeth Ann fell against the window. So hard, the latch gave away and the window swung open. She felt herself being pulled out ... out ... out into the night. She grabbed the side of the window frame with her free hand, grabbing hard ... for her life.

The bedroom door crashed open, the lights flashed on and, instantly, all was quiet except for Elizabeth Ann's choked sob as she slid to the floor by the window.

She heard her mother cry out and felt her father pick her up and carry her downstairs.

She couldn't answer the questions as they cleaned the blood from the claw marks on her shoulder and back, but she shook her head and mumbled, "No ... no ... it's not his fault ..." As horrified accusations were hurled at Sanderford, wherever he was hiding.

Then Elizabeth Ann took a deep, trembling breath and said, "The chair. The great-great-grandmother chair in the attic. ... Burn the chair ..." and the whole strange story came tumbling out.

By the time the story was finished, Elizabeth Ann's shoulder and back were softly wrapped in a clean, white bandage. They were all gathered in the kitchen and it was beginning to get light outside.

Elizabeth Ann stopped talking. She was exhausted. Her mother and father had listened and now sat with her in silence. After a few long minutes, her father rose. He went upstairs to the attic and brought down the dainty, dusty rocking-chair.

He carried it across the kitchen and out through the back door to the garden, where he put it down. Then he brought old newspapers out of the garage and, one by one, crumpled the sheets and tucked them under the chair.

Mother and daughter stood together, holding hands as they watched through the doorway. Elizabeth Ann's father struck a match and lit the papers in several places. The tiny flames licked around the seat of the great-great-grandmother rocker. It was very old, very dry, and the flames leaped on to it, consuming it quickly as the three of them stood, transfixed, watching the smoke curl into the morning sky.

Elizabeth Ann felt a soft tickle on her leg and looked down. Sanderford was with them, watching too, rubbing himself gently against Elizabeth Ann's leg and rumbling loudly with loving purrs.

THE MODEL

by James Turner

IT was hardly a doll's house. It was too big for that; it was too big for Serena's bedroom and her playroom, two steps down from the bedroom, was so full of toys and her piano that no one even considered it being put there. In fact, being a model of her home, Dockacre House, it had not been made for Serena at all, but as part of the historical Festival being held in the town at the beginning of July.

For whatever else it was, Dockacre House went back to the time of Elizabeth I, and was one of the oldest houses in the town. It was five-gabled and extensively modernised in Georgian times. Naturally, with so old a house, it was reputed to be haunted, though there was now no one living who could swear to having seen a ghost. Secret passages were said to lead from the house to either the church of St. Mary or to the eleventh-century castle. Someone once described it thus: "On the steep slope of the hill, clinging to its side, was the quaintest conceivable house—a long, narrow range of gables, roof and walls encased in small, slate-like armour. The foundations of the houses in the street above are higher than the tops of the chimneys." Dockacre was still a most secret house, enfolded by trees and bearing its age like a basilisk. Time winked from its chimneys like an old man; the lichens on its roofs were fingered with age, and the mulberry tree at one corner of the house was bowed with ancient memories.

The model of the house was, obviously, quite new. It was kept in an empty, rarely-visited room under one of the gables, ready to be brought out for the Festival and the showing of the real house. It had been finished over a fortnight before by a local carpenter. Serena had helped her mother to furnish it not only with tiny pieces of furniture but also with small figures of people, models of actual people who had once lived in the house.

"I wonder, Mummy," Serena asked, flicking her long, light brown hair out of her eyes, "whether this model is haunted, too, like the house itself?"

"Don't be absurd," her mother replied, too rushed with Festival preparations to bother much with her daughter. "It's only an old bit of wood and paint. You'd better go and practise your scales or you won't be ready for your lesson tomorrow."

Serena—not really interested in Nicholas and Elizabeth Herle, former owners of the house, who had died in the 1700s, and about whose persons the tales of haunting clung—ran off to do her mother's bidding. Death, at the age of ten, really did not mean much in terms of human beings. Yet, how unhappy she had been when her dog Buster died! Yes, but people, and so long ago? That was different. All you had was a churchyard full of ornate stones and flaky slates which sometimes had funny verses on them and made wonderful places for hide-and-seek on the way back from school. She had heard the story—of how Nicholas Herle had killed his wife Elizabeth by locking her up in what was now Serena's bedroom because she had gone mad, and she died there, or else he had shot her on the stairs—so many times that it was no more than any other story in the books in her playroom which she often read to her teddy bear, Percy.

Yet, by an odd quirk, if she didn't believe in the Herles, she did believe in the model house. It was large, as befitted the largeness of Dockacre House itself. Made of egg-boxes and papered to look exactly like the original, its windows opened and shut and the whole front swung out on hinges to reveal rooms full of tiny replicas of period furniture, early Georgian chairs and tables, and small squares of modern carpet laid in the two principal rooms. For the rest, the floors were bare or, as in the kitchen quarters, laid with bits of rush matting.

Serena, in that week before the Festival began, came to believe in the model completely and, at times, when she was free from the piano and other chores she did for her mother and father, even lived her life in it. The model became for her much more of a reality than the house itself. She would explore its rooms in her mind, with affection, living a tiny Serena-life of some hundreds of years ago. Here, in this attic room, she became the mistress of the household, ordering the servants to do as they were told, even punishing the tiny models when she considered that they had been disobedient. So large was the model that she could put her hand into the room when the front was hinged open, rearranging the furniture and the doll-like figures of the people inhabiting them, to suit the particular story she was living in.

She liked best, of all these people, the fat cook who presided over the great kitchen fire, her sleeves rolled up, the suggestion of sweat on her face. She called her Mrs. Tompkins. She knew her well because her mother had allowed her to dress the little figure in mob cap and apron and to add tiny patches of red paint on her face before they put her in position in the model. And Mrs. Tompkins knew a thing or two, that was obvious. It was odd, Serena thought, even while she was dressing Mrs. Tompkins, how the little figure seemed to move in her hands.

As for the figures of Nicholas and Elizabeth Herle, seated at a round table in the drawingroom, she hardly regarded them at all. Her father, who ran an antique shop in the town, had found them in a box of old toys he had bought. He brought them back to Dockacre House the same evening. It was almost as if they had been made for the model house, so greatly did they resemble, in their miniature way, the pastel portraits of the real persons hanging in the diningroom. But to Serena, at that time, they were uninteresting, since they formed no part of the fantasy she was weaving about the model house.

When she sat on the floor in front of the model she would hum tunes to herself, mimic the cook and scold

D

the man who looked after the yard and picked the mulberries from the great tree, reputed to be four hundred years old, which was growing against the north side of the house. She was not even surprised when the figure of Mrs. Tompkins turned from the roasting pig on the spit she was minding and said, quite clearly, "You watch out, Miss Serena, or you'll catch it. You mark my words. There's things as lie in wait."

Serena, quite unconscious of any danger to herself, was delighted. "You don't frighten me, Mrs. T.," she said, clapping her hands, "you're only an old wooden model. I'm flesh and blood. I could saw you in half in a second if I'd a mind to. It's you who'd better watch out, Mrs. Tompkins, dear, you'd better really. I'm bigger than you."

"Maybe, Miss Serena." The cook returned to her wooden posture before the fire, but not before she had added, "Maybe you're bigger, but you ain't wiser, nor so old, and I'm warning you."

Serena laughed with pleasure and suddenly snapped shut the hinged front of the model house. "There," she said, giving it a bang with her foot, "that'll shut you all up, you silly creatures. Goodnight."

She was so engrossed with the cook that she had not noticed that Nicholas Herle, only two inches high and wearing early-eighteenth-century dress, had turned in his chair to regard her, nor that Elizabeth, his wife, had actually risen in her seat. "Sit down, my dear," Nicholas said. "It's only Mrs. Tompkins scolding the yard man."

Serena didn't notice either that Nicholas took up the tiny replica flute on the table and began to play. So slight was the music, so wraith-like, that perhaps only Mrs. Tompkins heard it, just, above the spitting of the roast pig's crackling.

Life for Serena, in the Festival week, was exciting. Not only the dressing up, in costume, of practically everyone in the town so that you hardly knew your friends from the historical characters they chose to portray, such as the Blessed Cuthbert Mayne, the first Catholic martyr under Elizabeth I, who was hung, drawn and quartered in the town in 1571, or the Quaker, George Fox, who was imprisoned in the town gaol in 1656; not only the plays and the concerts and the organ recitals and poetry readings in the church, but also the fact that everyone came to see the inside of her home, Dockacre House. It was almost as if the townspeople seized this chance of at last seeing what was going on, what the Colonel, her father, was doing with the property, how well he and his wife were restoring the house. Indeed, to many it was refreshing to find a man who was prepared to preserve a building, unlike others who were mainly interested in pulling down the beauty of the town to make way for supermarkets, cash-and-carry stores, or car parks.

They came in great crowds once the Colonel opened the house and Serena, her little face peeping out of the banisters of the main staircase, listened to the capable lecture her father was giving before conducting parties of sightseers round the house. After three days of intensive activity, she knew most of it by heart. She was exceedingly proud of living in so famous a house and, now, she often looked at the pastel portraits, hanging in the dining-room, of Nicholas and Elizabeth Herle. Nicholas had been a barrister and his wife the daughter of a former rector of Northcote, the Reverend Ackland. She decided that, on the whole, she didn't much like Nicholas. Elizabeth was different. For her she felt a pity so intense that, at times, she thought the lady in the picture was aware of her sympathy.

Now, from her position on the staircase, she was getting a tiny bit bored as her father's voice came up to her. The crowd of listening people was very still, a testimony to the excellence of the story the Colonel was telling.

"It is known from records," he was saying, "that Nicholas Herle was twice Mayor of the town in the years 1716 and 1721. He was also sometime High Sheriff of Cornwall." He paused a moment and turned round from the table, pointing to the pictures on the wall. "These two portraits have hung in the diningroom at Dockacre House since before Elizabeth Herle died, in 1714," he said, "and there is a monument to her in St. Mary Magdalen church here which reads, 'Depart ye life 25 Dec. 1714 by starvation or other unlawful mean'. The burial records of the church for that period show that she was buried on the 28th December, 1714." He turned back again and addressed his audience.

Serena was very tempted to start pulling faces at him, in order to make him laugh, for there was no doubt about it, he was being very serious indeed. Instead, she turned her head sideways and began chewing her long hair and playing with the period ribbons of her Festival dress. She considered that she looked rather pretty in the smock her mother had chosen for her.

"There are two stories concerning the death of Elizabeth Herle," she heard her father saying through her absorption in her dress. "The first is that she went mad and Nicholas locked her up in an upstairs room and starved her, the then cure for madness. Unfortunately she was kept too long in confinement and she died."

Just at this moment Serena's dog Spot, who had replaced Buster, ran up the stairs and began licking her bare legs. She bent down and hugged him, thinking how awful it must be to be starved, trying to imagine herself longing for food twice as badly as she did sometimes at school. She hugged Spot all the closer as her father went on. "The second story is that he accidentally, or intentionally, shot his wife on the staircase. A local inhabitant reports having seen a large bloodstain on the main staircase just about where my daughter Serena is now standing looking at us."

The crowd of people turned to gaze at her. A sigh of satisfied fright at the idea of blood rose from them. They were determined to have their money's worth. Serena, not in the least put out, smiled back at them, recognising her friends under their Festival disguises.

"I'm sorry to disappoint you all," the Colonel went on, "but I can't show you any blood since the staircase treads were removed a few years ago and all evidence has gone for ever."

Serena had the exciting idea of buying a bottle of red ink and spilling it at the spot where she was standing. Suddenly her hair began to stand on end as she explored the wonderful thought. Perhaps she might even frighten her father, though this she doubted; he was so strong and fine a man and, from his being a soldier, knew all about blood and swords and wounds and entrails and bodies without heads and bleeding stumps and . . . the *enemy*. So it wouldn't be any good, he'd soon spot it was red ink and she'd be sent to wash it off.

"It is known that Nicholas Herle died on 4th August, 1728, at Hampstead and his ghost is reputed to be seen usually in the main hall. He also plays a flute when a death is about to occur in the house. The flute he plays is one that no mortal can now play, for one end has been blocked up and it has been made into a walkingstick." The Colonel now handed the walkingstick flute to the nearest of his listeners and it was passed round. "The tune he plays is an old English madrigal, the first verse of which goes as follows:

'Since first I saw your face
  I resolved
To honour and renown you;
If now I be disdained,
  I wish
My heart had never known you.'

"It has always been a tradition that every owner of Dockacre House hands to his successor a walkingstick. Over the years the collection has grown to thirteen, including the 'flute-stick'. These sticks, kept in a sack in the attic, are subject to the supernatural; for if they are not put away in a particular order, they will, with much rattling, sort themselves out into the correct order. They are a curious collection ranging from a swordstick to one with a detachable knob capable of carrying poison. And further," the Colonel added, "the exact order of the sticks is a secret handed on from one owner to the next."

Serena fled up the stairs when the lecture was over. Her father began to take the party round the house. A shuffling of feet could be heard, the long house was ringing with the noise. Serena dashed into her playroom and shut the door. She knew that her father would not disturb her. He might show the guest-room under the roof where the walkingsticks were kept when they were not on show, but her two little rooms were sacrosanct except to personal friends of herself and her parents.

She sat down at the piano, her teddy-bear, Percy, on the top, and began, very softly, to play him a lullaby. It was only noon but, in a few minutes, his eyes began to close, his arms to slide down to his sides.

"Well," she said gently, getting up from the piano stool, "that worked, didn't it, Percy? Now you can sleep till I want you again, old bear, dear, naughty old bear.

I love you very dearly, you know that, don't you?" And giving him a huge, wet kiss she laid him down in an easy chair. A few minutes later, amidst the shuffling of feet on the staircase where once had been bloodstains, Percy's snores filled her playroom. Serena smiled to herself and went into her little bedroom and stood at the window looking out at the mulberry tree, its dark brown, thick, rough bark dappled with the sun pouring in through the canopy of leathery, heart-shaped leaves. In the very slight breeze their shiny upper surfaces were like a thousand mirrors. She thought she could see her reflection in every one of them. She had completely forgotten Mrs. Tompkins and the model house which, at this moment, were being admired by the sightseers.

She never knew if it was part of the Festival, a tradition of the town, or whether it really happened to her. Indeed, the atmosphere of the town was so charged with what might be called "Festival fever" that anything might have happened. She did not really think about it at all. All she knew was that it was midnight for, as she stood in the street in the shadow of the old town gaol, she heard the clock on the church strike twelve. She was not in the least afraid. Just the reverse—a wonderful sense of happiness filled her little body. Nor was she surprised to find herself wearing only pyjamas and dressing-gown.

She was standing looking at Eagle House, and when she perceived that the stone figure of Britannia, which stood on the apex of the roof, and the two eagles on the gate-posts, were no longer in their positions then she knew why she had come. Her little body thrilled with pleasure. So, it was true then! But before she could exclaim with wonder she felt a touch on her shoulder. A warmth, over and above the hot summer night, was surrounding her. She was enveloped in this comforting warmth as in a spiritual cloak. She turned and smiled at the man who had come up beside her.

"Oh, it's you Mr. Fox," she said. She knew his face well from reading histories of the town. She knew how, years ago, he had suffered here, in the gaol. "And who is your friend behind you?"

George Fox (she noticed that his body was illuminated with a curious light which had something to do with the warmth she was feeling) moved aside a little to introduce a small gentleman who was hovering in the shadows. "Why, Serena, this is my dear friend Father Cuthbert Mayne. I expect you know we both suffered for our religious beliefs in that gaol behind you, now, thanks be to God, fallen into ruin. Cuthbert, alas, suffered far more than I. But then he's a Catholic. I think they were hated and feared more than we Quakers. How anyone could hate or fear Cuthbert I don't know."

"Yes," Serena replied, and now the light was stronger. It was almost, she thought, as if she could see through them. "Yes, I do know and I've often shed tears for you both. My schoolmistress often talks about you. It must have been horrible and I hate the people who made you suffer so." She moved a little closer, utterly confident. "Do you think I might just kiss your hands? I'd like very much to comfort you, and indeed," she added primly and decidedly, "if I had been alive then and not now, I would have brought you soup and bread. It wouldn't have been much but it would have warmed you a little." She stamped her foot. "I think people were horrid in those days."

Father Cuthbert Mayne smiled gently and leaned forward, holding out his hand, on which was a great, shining ring, for Serena to kiss, which she did with exquisite demureness and simplicity. He was wearing a black cassock-like robe and a huge crucifix hung from a gold chain about his neck. His eyes were bright and clear.

"Yes," he said, "I suppose people were different then, although I have my doubts. I don't suppose they knew any better. And, happily, we had God to sustain us. Of course, George and I know now that it was the same God we suffered for, even if we didn't see eye to eye in the old days."

Before he could say another word there was a slight commotion in the street before them.

"Forgive me," Serena said, turning round. "I've come to see the eagles and Britannia return from the river. I've never seen them before, though, of course, everyone else has. I expect you know how each night they are supposed to come down from their pedestals and go to the river for a drink?" She was licking her lips in anticipation.

"Yes." Mr. Fox moved to her side as if to protect her. "We watch Britannia come down from the roof almost every night, with her birds. They're glad to be free from their pedestals for a bit, I'm sure. Must get very stiff up there all day, don't you think? You see, Cuthbert and I know all about being stiff, shut up as we were in that foul place. Cuthbert was far more patient than I, though."

Then suddenly, in the moonlight, they came, very proudly, one each side of Britannia in her helmet, up the road, back to Eagle House. Serena, clapping her hands with delight, thought that they gave her a wicked smile as they flew up to the pedestals on each side of the gate and came to rest. One of them shuffled about a great deal on its perch and began to preen its breast feathers.

Britannia had ascended to the roof of the house and was looking severely at her birds. Serena was watching her from the street and, if the truth be told, she was rather in

105

love with the imperious figure with shield in one hand and drawn sword in the other.

"Right, boys," Britannia called down to the eagles below her, rather as if they were her sons. "That will do for tonight. No more noise. I'm going to bang my shield once and I want to see all of us completely still afterwards, until tomorrow night."

Serena was delighted as the sword came clanging down on the shield. She just had time to hear a voice behind her murmur, "Do take care, child. And, remember, if you need us, we are always here," and the great booming ring of Britannia's shield sounded over the town.

She turned and found herself alone in the street. A moment later two long-haired youths on motorcycles roared round the corner and shot off down the hill, past the museum, fairly blasting the quiet of the night. Serena knew it was no good staying any longer. Mr. Fox and Father Mayne would be gone, probably walking in Castle Park and arguing about the nature of God, unseen by anyone but her. The eagles and Britannia were no longer anything but painted lead sculpture.

She trotted back to Dockacre House and her bed. She noticed that two mulberry leaves had somehow blown into her bedroom and were lying on her pillow. She went to the window. To her surprise she saw that the tree was covered in a moving mass of caterpillars. The high moon which had allowed her to see the eagles return from the river and the faces of George Fox and Cuthbert Mayne was now penetratingly bright. It was illuminating the caterpillars with a luminous light. The weight of their green and white bodies seemed to be swaying the whole tree which almost appeared to be sinking under it.

As she stood and watched she was suddenly conscious that the silkworms were as aware of her as she was of them. They were creating (as had Mr. Fox and Father

106

Mayne) an extraordinary warmth of protection about her. "Serena, Serena," she thought she heard the tiny voices calling to her. She opened the windows wide and looked into the huge eyes of the silkworms. She opened her arms and allowed the silken gossamer of their guardianship to float about her. "Yes, yes," she heard herself whisper, her heart full of thankfulness that, whatever her danger (perhaps Mrs. Tompkins was right?), she now had three protectors—Mr. Fox, Father Mayne and the silkworms.

She turned back to her bed. Now the caterpillars had moved from the mulberry leaves and appeared to be standing guard on the windowsill, their eyes large, aware, moving from side to side, the sentinels of nature against the unnatural.

Serena smiled sleepily. She knew all the sounds which a house as old as Dockacre makes at night, had made all the years down from Tudor times. Now, in the stillness, the moonlight dying away down the town sky, stepping from chimneys to first-floor windows and then to pavements and so gone, she heard the sound of a flute. It was far away at first and then, as she lay half asleep, it seemed to be outside the door of her playroom. "Oh, Nicholas," she murmured, and turned over into sleep. "It's lovely, lovely. Play it again." And although she did not know it, her voice was that of a grown woman. At dawn the silkworms left the window of her bedroom and curled themselves into secret places in the tree's bark.

Of course, if she remembered it at all the next morning, it was as a dream. She ran into the garden, in the brilliant sunlight, to the mulberry tree. It was standing firm beside the wall overlooking the new road which had once been part of her father's garden. There was no sign of the silkworms.

It was the last night of the Festival. The town's houses were full of people giving parties, and Serena had been allowed to stay up for the party her father was giving. "Just this once," she begged her mother, and permission was granted. "There'll be a lot of noise, I expect, and you wouldn't sleep anyway."

By ten-thirty all the guests had gone. A great storm of wind and rain was raging over the whole of Cornwall and in it Dockacre House was creaking in its ancient bones. The trees in the drive were whipping the rain in flat sheets against the window-panes. When her mother kissed her goodnight, and as she began to tumble into sleep, Serena had the odd feeling that her mother had not left the room at all. Her mother, or someone else, was there in the room with her, filling its tiny space with her whole body.

And when suddenly she woke to the sound of flute music she was certain of someone else in the room. Only now it was no longer her mother. The wind was still blowing with great force, as if to scour the town of all Festival mess—papers, ice-cream cartons and other litter— when Serena opened her bedroom door and followed the music of the flute across the landing and into the room under the roof where the model house had been returned when the Festival finally closed.

Now, when she stood looking at it, compelled by the music, she saw that the lights (from secret torch-bulbs her father had installed) were blazing in every room. The model was alive, quivering almost with life—Serena thought she could see even the polish on the tiny furniture. It was swelling, vibrating in an alarming manner, the hinged front door open so that she could see into every room.

And then the tiny figure of Elizabeth Herle was standing outside the model. As Serena watched, the figure began to grow in stature, to take on life, so that she could see the rise and fall of Elizabeth's breast as she breathed. In a moment the figure was life-size, standing over Serena, a kind of pity in its eyes, breathing into her mouth, holding her little body in its sharp-fingered hands, infusing itself into Serena, living on her life, enormous compared with the model figure which had been seated at the miniature table.

Serena was unable to move, her eyes fixed (as if this was determined for her) on the figure of Nicholas Herle, still small, still doll-like yet, but already risen from his chair, the flute to his lips. With one last despairing effort she managed to kick the front of the model shut. It was her last action as the girl Serena. From them on she was Elizabeth Herle. Yet she waited, feeling her body swelling, her voice contracting, her hands extending beyond her ten years, and her feet aching with hugeness.

The slamming-to of the model door was no escape. Her eyes, now capable of seeing twice as much as before, opened wide as she heard the front door of the model creaking slowly open. Elizabeth Herle was moving within her. "It's not my fault," she was crying, the words coming from Serena's throat, "it's not my fault. I was never mad, except through hunger. And now he'll kill me."

Serena's body was suddenly limp with an appalling desire for food. Mrs. Tompkins, she saw, was looking out of the kitchen window. She was leering at Serena and swinging a succulent leg of pork in her hands, shouting, "I told you to watch out, Mrs. Herle, madam, didn't I? I told you you'd catch it if you kept crying out for food." She laughed obscenely. "Now you're going to cop it, you are."

The flute music, from inside the model, was swelling and increasing as she saw Nicholas Herle come out of the open front door on to the floorboards of the attic. He had a pistol stuck in his waist-band. He was looking at her, at Elizabeth, his mad, starving wife, within her. He suddenly pulled the leg of pork out of Mrs. Tompkin's hands and flung it away. A moment later the flute music filled the entire attic and, as Serena fled, unable to escape the fearful possession of Elizabeth, Nicholas followed her with an awful inevitability.

There was no escape, in the real house, as she fled from door to door and so to the main staircase with Nicholas, her husband, after her. She heard (as the real Elizabeth must have heard in 1714) the collection of sticks rattling away in the guest-room, and she ran headlong down the stairs, the dead Elizabeth's fear, now very real, impelling her to escape. For now she was the Elizabeth of all those years ago, her agony of terror upon her.

Always Nicholas was behind her, his tread heavy on the bare boards, always his music one step away from her. She knew that when the flute stopped he would take out the pistol at his waist and she would die.

She had reached the third step from the bottom when the music stopped. A pistol shot rang out, shattering the quiet of the house and, in a last desperate effort at sanity, she threw herself forward into the arms of the man waiting at the foot of the stairs.

"Father, Father!" she was screaming when Cuthbert Mayne advanced across the hall and caught her. In his right hand a large and ornate crucifix was gleaming with light and he was murmuring to Serena, "There is nothing to be afraid of now, Elizabeth. Nothing Nicholas can do to you. You are safe with us." At that moment she did not know if Cuthbert Mayne was referring to himself and Mr. Fox or to himself and the crucifix held above his head.

With a sigh of relief she sank back on his knees on the floor. The fearful figure of Nicholas Herle peered

She ran headlong down the stairs . . .

down at them and then slowly retreated. Serena felt her body melt to the size of a small girl and called out again, "Father, Father!" and woke to find her head pillowed on the Colonel's knees and her mother beside her.

"Darling, darling," her mother was saying, "no one is going to hurt you. You've been dreaming. Now let Daddy carry you to bed again. All those silly people you were babbling about, Nicholas Herle and Elizabeth, were all dead centuries ago. It's all the excitement of the Festival and everyone dressing up, and this terrible storm on top of it."

The Colonel was not so sure. He was disturbed. The night before, when he carried Serena to her room and sat with her till she was asleep, he had seen the bloodstains on the third stair, bright on the carpet. Her mother had very gently examined her daughter's body but there was no trace of blood. She sat in the tiny bedroom for the rest of the night. When she came out of the room to breakfast she saw that the Colonel had covered the third step with a piece of sacking.

"We shall have to tell her," he said. "At the moment I can find no way of getting rid of the bloodstains and she's bound to spot them. However, I have been able to remove the pistol."

"Pistol?" his wife asked, alarmed. "What pistol?"

"It was lying there against the wall at the top of the stairs. I saw it first when I was carrying Serena to her bed last night. "Look." He took the weapon from his jacket pocket. "Look at the initials on that silver plate behind the trigger. N.H. 1700."

"So she wasn't dreaming after all?"

"It seems like it. And there's another thing. Rather sad really. The mulberry tree was blown down in the storm last night. I suppose it was so very old it couldn't stand against the wind."

"She was talking a little in her sleep," her mother said, thinking more about Serena than of the old tree. "Just about dawn. She was mumbling about the model, you know, in the attic."

"My dear," the Colonel said firmly. He was a man of quick decisions. "I've seen to that, I promise you. We ought to have been aware that it had an attraction for Serena. She was always playing with it. No. I put an axe through it and burnt it. There was one funny thing about it, though. The figures of Nicholas and Elizabeth Herle, you know, the ones I found in the shop and brought here, were missing. I looked most carefully. Ah, and that fat cook figure which Serena helped you dress. Nowhere to be seen, any of 'em."

At that moment Serena herself, completely recovered, ran down the stairs and into the breakfast room.

"Daddy," she kissed him, "why on earth have you covered up the bloodstains on the stairs? Poor, poor, Elizabeth. You know, after what she suffered, I think she was glad to be dead."

The Colonel looked at his wife. "Sit down, Serena, and have your breakfast. Afterwards I'll get the doctor to look you over. Give you a few pills to stop you sleep-walking."

Serena sprang up. "Oh, no, Daddy, there'll be no need of that! Nicholas and Elizabeth are happy now, and I'm quite all right. Besides, I've never sleep-walked in my life." She ran to the door. "I've something I must do before I have breakfast," she said. "I shan't be long."

"Where are you going? Serena, come back." The Colonel was alarmed and half out of his chair.

"Oh, there's no danger," Serena laughed with happiness.

"I'm only going up the hill to thank someone for something." And she was gone.

Actually she found them waiting for her. The church clock was striking nine when she saw their gentle figures beside the gaol, outlined by the very green grass of Castle Park. She ran, first of all to Cuthbert Mayne and hugged him, and then to Mr. Fox who enfolded her in the great cloak he was wearing.

"Oh, thank you, thank you," she stammered out.

"My dear child, we would never have let you be hurt, you know that, don't you? It was just that it was the only way."

"Of course. I always knew you were my friends." Serena was logical and exact. "But it isn't for myself that I'm thanking you."

Mr. Fox was taken aback. "For whom, then?"

"For her, for poor Elizabeth Herle. Now she's free for ever, isn't she? She will not have to suffer again, will she? Or be a ghost and haunt our home? And Nicholas, too, perhaps? Only he's a man, isn't he, and can look after himself? Besides, he's got his flute and poor Elizabeth had nothing."

Mr. Fox stood back against the grey wall of the gaol. "Perhaps all three of us ought to be thanked, Serena," he said, "you as much as us. We all helped one way or the other. Poor Elizabeth—as you say, she's waited a long time." He turned to look behind him. "Ah, I see Cuthbert has gone on. He's a bit shy of being thanked, I fear, and prefers to be alone. But it was most considerate of you to come." He put out his hand and rested it on her fair hair, a little girl and a tall man beside the gaol wall.

The Colonel, however, as he came up the hill to fetch his daughter back to breakfast, saw only a small child, her head bowed, filled with happiness. The sunlight, after the night of storm, seemed very brilliant at the spot where she was standing.

"Daddy," she said, when he reached her, "I really am very fond of Mr. Fox. And I believe Father Mayne likes me a little, only he's terribly shy. It's sad."

"Yes," the Colonel said, raising his eyebrows a little. "You have some good friends, Serena; I can see that. I'm happy for you. But now I think it's time you came and had breakfast. We don't want Mummy to worry, do we?"

ROOM AT THE INN

by Sydney J. Bounds

SUNSET laid a sheen of blood over bleak and desolate moorland. Wind came in great gusts, blowing the two cycles across the empty road, carrying with it an icy lash of rain.

Jane Black and her younger sister, Penny, on a cycling tour of Cornwall, were somewhere on Bodmin Moor.

"This," Jane said a trifle grimly, "is no longer funny. We'll have to stop and cape up."

The two girls, both in jeans and wind-cheaters, got off their bikes, unrolled yellow oilskins and put them on. When they started off again, the wind howled in fury and threatened to blow them right off the road. The sun had almost gone and dark clouds piled high in a granite sky.

"It's a pity we ever left the main road," Penny gasped, head down and wrestling with her machine to keep it upright. "Any idea where we are?" Her words were whipped away.

"What was that?" Jane shouted.

"I said . . . oh, never mind. . . ."

The sky split and rain deluged down.

"We'll never get a tent up in this," Jane said. "Have to press on till we find some kind of shelter."

They were miles from any village and there wasn't a house, or even a car, in sight. Jane had the eerie notion they were lone survivors, cut off from the rest of the world.

Heads down, braced against the wind, they cycled through drenching rain.

"A light!" Penny pointed, and fell off her bike.

Jane braked. "You all right?"

"Of course I am. . . . Look over there."

To the left, standing back from the road and on the crest of a tor, was the shadow of a house with a yellow light burning.

"Come on," Jane said briskly. "No one can refuse us shelter tonight."

They pushed their bikes towards the building and entered a yard; outhouses cut off some of the wind. They put their bikes out of the rain, unstrapped their saddlebags and made a run for the door of the house. A dark sign swung creakily overhead.

"It's an inn—and they won't hear us in this lot."

Boldly, Jane pushed open the door and stepped into a stone-flagged passage. "Anyone home?"

Just off the passage was a small bar with bottles and casks; an oil lamp burned here. The rest of the house was in darkness, silent. Her voice echoed in emptiness.

A girl, not much older than Jane, appeared out of the gloom. Her skirt touched the floor; a shawl draped her shoulders and her hair was done in ringlets.

"My uncle's away just now——"

116

"Can you put us up for the night?" Jane said quickly. "We're wet through."

"And cold. And hungry," Penny added.

The girl looked doubtful. "My uncle won't like——" She hesitated. "But I can't turn you away in this weather. Yes, you can stay the night."

"Thanks. We're cycling round Cornwall and——"

"Cycling?" The girl looked blank, then said: "I'm called Jessica. Come through to the kitchen and get out of those wet things."

Jane and Penny followed her along a dark passage to a kitchen with an oil lamp and stove. They stripped and Jessica brought them each a blanket to wrap round them.

They sat at a plain wood table, on hard-backed chairs, and Jessica poured hot soup into bowls. "I'm afraid there isn't much else," she said. "We don't get many people stopping here."

"Soup's lovely," Penny said. "I feel warm and sleepy already."

Jessica lit a candle. "This way, then."

They went up a flight of wooden stairs, the boards creaking, to another passage with doors leading off. Jessica opened one. "In here."

Penny saw that the next door, the last in the passage, was closed and padlocked. "What's in there?" she asked, curious.

Jane said quickly: "It's none of your business," and pushed her into their bedroom.

The walls were plaster, the boards bare. There was an old-fashioned double-bed and grime on a window which looked as if it had not been opened for years.

Jessica handed Jane a large iron key, one end of which was cross-shaped. "Lock your door," she said solemnly. "Don't open it no matter what you hear tonight."

"What are we likely to hear?" Penny asked promptly.

But Jessica shut the door on them.

Jane put the key in the lock and turned it, felt the bed. "Damp—lucky we've got our sleeping bags."

"Pretty primitive, the whole place," Penny sniffed. "And Jessica—I think she's weird."

Snug in her sleeping bag, the last thing Jane heard was the drumming of the rain.

She woke reluctantly, becoming slowly aware of a hand shaking her shoulder and Penny's urgent voice: "Something funny's going on."

"Not funny . . . go back to sleep."

"Oh, wake up, Jane! Please!"

Jane realised that the wind and rain had stopped, that drunken singing rose from below. Penny pushed a wristwatch before her eyes.

"It's three in the morning—and just look out here!" Penny crossed to the window and pointed down.

Jane wriggled out of her sleeping bag and padded over bare boards. A full moon hung in the sky. Wheels rumbled noisily as a train of horse-drawn wagons pulled into the yard below. She heard coarse laughter follow some of the words.

The men with the wagons were dressed in jerseys and dark, flaring trousers; some had knives and one an eye-patch. Their leader, big and bearded, cursed them.

"A villainous lot," Penny said. "What d'you suppose they're doing?"

Large boxes were dragged from the wagons and let fall, heavily, on the ground. Staggering, the men carried them, one by one, through the inn porch.

Presently, there came a bumping sound as the boxes were hauled up the stairs. Boots echoed in the passage. Wood scraped as the boxes were dragged past the girls' bedroom. Iron rattled.

"The locked room next door," Penny whispered excitedly. "Do you think they're smugglers?"

"Don't be silly," Jane said, "and keep quiet." Remembering what Jessica had told them, she added: "Anyway, it's nothing to do with us."

Heavy footfalls came along the passage, stopped outside their door. A hand rattled the door-handle and a harsh voice demanded: "Anyone in here?"

Jane clamped a hand over Penny's mouth, and Jessica's voice sounded in the passage:

"Two guests, caught by the weather. They're locked in, and drugged."

The man laughed unpleasantly. "Lucky for them. Show their noses tonight and they'll get their throats cut."

Penny shivered. "I don't like this," she whispered. "I'm scared."

There were more scraping noises as boxes were shoved into the room next door. The men made several trips, then the door was locked again.

Boots trod the bare boards, going downstairs. The last pair paused outside the bedroom . . .

"Don't even breathe," Jane whispered, hugging her sister.

Finally, the last man moved away and the passage was silent again. There came a creak of harness and a clop-clop of hooves.

Cautiously, Jane peered from the window. She saw the wagon train leaving the inn, heading out across the moonlit moor.

"It's all right, Penny, they've gone now."

The inn seemed strangely quiet as the two girls wriggled deep into sleeping bags and, despite a sense of unease, both were soon asleep.

Jane woke with the sun in her eyes. Her hip and shoulder ached from lying on hard and uneven ground. Ground?

Suddenly she remembered where she was and sat up. There was no roof, no walls—only a few flagstones scattered around. She lay on the ground with the moor stretching away into the distance.

Penny was still asleep, curled up in her sleeping bag, and their bikes lay propped against a stone some yards away.

Jane, realizing with a chill that she lay in the ruins of the inn, pinched herself. She was sure she was awake. . . .

She shook Penny and her sister woke suddenly. "They haven't come back——?"

Penny looked at the ruins in disbelief. "It couldn't have been a dream. It was too real!"

"Our clothes . . . lucky there's no one about to see us."

Jane was sure their clothes lay where the kitchen stove would have been. Abruptly, she said, "Come on, let's get away from here."

They dressed quickly and rolled their sleeping bags, and as Jane shook hers, something metallic fell out. A rusty iron key with a cross at one end.

EDWARD

by Mary Danby

THE gulls wheeled in a smooth arc, their shrill clamour harsh on the damp sea breeze. One by one, they broke away to swoop and settle, ruffling their salty feathers with abrupt dignity, scanning with pebble-black eyes the curling waters of the bay. The hurt one stood alone on a cliff-top post, holding out his broken wing like a beggar's palm.

Edward called to him in a thin, high voice. "Here! Here little gull!" But the bird maintained its precarious balance and took no heed. Edward would have liked to make a pet of the bird with a broken wing, to teach him to come to the window for scraps of bread—perhaps even to sit on his hand while Edward fixed a splint to the battered wing. He turned his pale face back to the room and watched a spider make tentative threads between the roof beams. Soon, Aunt Lavinia would come with her cobweb brush to send the spider scuttling back to the dark corners, its unfinished miracle now limply tangled on the coarse hairs of the brush.

It was the same for Edward. All his life, whenever he had wanted to do anything, whenever he had begun to take an interest in something, it had been taken away from him. He had a weak heart, the doctors said, and should not be allowed to exert himself in any way. The battledore and shuttlecock he had been given on his ninth birthday lay on the floor of his cupboard, unused. The diabolo he had made out of papier-maché and string had been hidden by his careful aunt. "It'll bring on one of your attacks. You know it will," she had said. "Just think what your Mama and Papa would say."

He hadn't seen his mother and father for almost two months—not since his baby sister had been born and he had been sent to live with Aunt Lavinia on the east coast. Soon after he had arrived, he had been seized by fainting fits while walking along the cliffs, and Aunt Lavinia's doctor had said he was to stay sitting quietly in his room. He could open the windows, they said, and breathe in the good sea air. Any further exercise might prove fatal.

Edward was used to restrictions. He didn't fight them, as other children might have done, he simply did what he was told and smiled gently while his aunt fussed around

121

him, reading unsuitable stories to him, upsetting his jigsaw puzzles and disarranging his shell collection. There were other things in Edward's life.

There were the magic cloud-places, where he dwelt on sunless days, the floating mansions and drifting plains where his feet made no noise and his ears heard whispered secrets from the rain-spirits. There were the gold-green caverns under the waves and the cool-eyed monsters who swam with him there, tending their gardens of sharp-toothed sea-flowers. When the winds came, he ran with them through the cool sedge-grasses beside the cliff path, and saw the nesting plovers turning their backs to the swift-blowing sand.

Early in the mornings, he saw the dark cormorants diving for mackerel, seagulls following shoals of herring, far out where the trawling schooners rode against the horizon. This was Edward's world. His small body took its humble place in the raftered bedroom, but his mind reached out like a great seabird to the sky and the waves.

Aunt Lavinia came fussing up the stairs with Edward's evening bowl of warm chicken broth. "My, my!" she said, closing the window, "I do believe we might be in for a storm." She settled her nephew into his bed, lit the candle and drew the curtains close.

Edward drank his broth dutifully, while Aunt Lavinia tidied up his books and toys, dusted his washstand and straightened his patchwork counterpane. Then she saw the spider's web and hurried out to the landing for her cobweb brush. "Not in my house, you don't," she said, bustling back into the room and sweeping the rafters with brisk flourishing movements. "Nasty, dirty thing."

"But he catches flies," protested Edward.

"Yes, and they're nasty, dirty things, too. I won't have

them. If you've finished your broth, you can say your prayers, then you'll be fast asleep before the storm comes."

But Edward liked storms. As soon as Aunt Lavinia has kissed him goodnight, blown out his candle and called from the door, as she always did, "Eyes shut tight, no chink of light, and God will guard thee through this night," he sat up in bed and pulled back one of the curtains. Outside, the sky was darkening, and thunderclouds gathered over the heavy sea. The moon edged silently into view, then hid again as a faraway rumble rolled majestically through the heavens.

Edward drew the counterpane up to his chin and shivered with pleasure. Lightning lit up the gaunt headland for an instant, and suddenly the thunder was nearer. How it boomed! How it roared over their heads like some great warrior come to conquer the world. Then the first raindrops clattered on the roof and streaked down the window-pane. Rivers and tributaries met and divided in an endless flow. Now it seemed that the sky was split in two by the warrior's sword, unleashing a torrent of blinding water. The sea danced to its ceaseless drumming and the cliff grass bowed low before the onslaught. On into the night the great battle surged, until Edward finally flopped back on his pillow and allowed the tempest to lull his senses to sleep.

When he awoke, there was an uncanny stillness outside. He opened the window and felt the cool, damp freshness of the air. The sea was as flat as a table, and the sky a mild uniform grey. Birds began to stir and greet the day with calls to their companions, like survivors searching for lost mates. Aunt Lavinia was awake, too, and Edward could hear her clucking as she surveyed her ravaged garden from an upstairs window.

He read for a while a book about sailing ships and

wished he could sail the world like Captain Cook. He would climb the rigging and it would be like flying over the waves. The heavy sails would fill with a salty wind and carry him south to adventure.

But there were no adventures in Edward's life. There was only Aunt Lavinia with breakfast and a letter from his parents. The baby was slightly unwell, and Edward should remain at the coast for a few more weeks. "There," said Aunt Lavinia, "isn't that nice? I'll have you all to myself for a little while longer. And my goodness, we'll have to see what we can do about lessons, won't we?" Edward gave a bleak sigh, but Aunt Lavinia continued: "I'll go this very morning and talk to Mr. Middleditch— he's the schoolmaster in the village. Perhaps he would be willing to give you some private tuition."

Edward did not want a tutor. He wasn't interested in anything that might force his mind to stay caged-up indoors. He wanted to learn about life outside, not the mathematics and English grammar which Mr. Middleditch would doubtless consider more important.

When Aunt Lavinia had gone, he sighed and turned to the open window. The injured gull was back, sitting on its post. Edward threw down a piece of his bread and butter, but it fell too near the house and a starling flew out of a bush and snatched it up.

"I'm going now," Aunt Lavinia called up the stairs. "Mind you eat all your good breakfast." Her little buttoned boots went click-click along the front path and out into the road.

The gull with the broken wing toppled off the post and gave a lurching hop back on to it. The poor thing looked ill and feeble and Edward wondered how it managed to catch its food. "Here gull!" he cried and threw down another piece of bread. This time it landed a few yards from the post, but before the bird could get to it, there was a tearing, sucking noise, and Edward saw the edge of the cliff begin to break up. Last night's torrential rain had soaked into the chalk, causing large areas of it to crumble, and the ground shook above the shifting mass. The gull on the post opened an alarmed beak before his perch tipped over, tumbling him to the beach in an avalanche of chalk and stones.

Where the post had been, there was now a broken gap, fringed with exposed roots and dusty foliage which clung lopsidedly to the chalk face for support. A network of open seams along the cliff top showed white through the tall grass and now and then a piece of chalk broke away to bounce gaily down to the sea.

Edward could not see the gull and tears blurred his gaze as he waited for the rest of the cliff to let go and take Aunt Lavinia's house down, down to the pebbled beach. Any movement now could start a landslide.

Leaning out of the window, Edward scanned the cliff path. Over to the left, laughing and twittering, a group of elegantly-dressed young ladies was advancing, picking flowers and waving at the distant schooners. There was an older woman with them, hurrying them along and pointing out interesting plants with her ribbon-tied parasol. Edward knew this was Miss Augusta Settle, taking the girls of the Academy on a nature walk.

But the cliff! In a few minutes they would be walking on the weak parts and the cliff would crumble beneath their weight. They would plummet, shrieking, to the beach below. They would die. Aunt Lavinia's house would topple. Edward would fall to the end of the earth.

His heart stopped beating for an anxious moment. He knew what he must do.

He eased himself carefully out of bed and crossed to the door, where he held on to the handle, catching his breath. Then he stumbled out to the landing and made for the head of the stairs. His heart was beating to a wild rhythm, making the blood pound in his temples. As he put his hands up to his head he missed his footing and fell heavily against the banister rail. The shock seemed to calm his heart and he stepped firmly down the rest of the stairs to the hall. As though in a far-off dream he found himself lifting the latch on the front door and running round the side of the house. The young ladies were quite close now, and seemed unaware of the danger ahead.

Edward called to them, "Stop! Stop! Oh please, stop!" But they chattered on past him, brushing against him with their wide skirts.

"Observe the sea pink," said Miss Augusta Settle. "It has another name, girls, and that is thrift. A virtue which, as you are all aware, is of prime importance in young ladies. Is that not so?"

"Yes, Miss Augusta," chorused the girls, turning their backs on Edward as he tugged feebly at their dresses. When they had finished inspecting the small flower, they moved on, and Edward knew now that he could not stop them. In a few more steps they would be upon the place and, even before they could see the danger, it would be too late. Why did they not heed him? Why, oh why did they not stop?

A high-pitched scream cut through the sea breezes, making the small party exchange frightened looks and turn towards the house. Seconds later, Aunt Lavinia was seen running out of the front gate, her bonnet askew and her cloak flapping crazily about her. "Miss Settle!" she cried frantically. "Girls!" And she fell into their flustered arms.

When they had calmed her, they heard how she had returned from her visit to Mr. Middleditch to find her nephew lying at the top of the stairs. "My Edward, my

They chattered on past him . ; ;

poor sick boy. So good. So sad. Ah, what am I to say to his dear, suffering mother?" Here she took out a small lace handkerchief and tried to blow her nose daintily. "Dead, you know. Quite dead."

The girls rustled like a bunch of dry leaves, gathering their skirts around them as a chill wind blew from the sea. Miss Augusta Settle said, "You were the soul of kindness to him, my dear, no one could have done more," and the two women looked towards Edward's resting place and grieved together.

When the moment came and the cliff finally, reluctantly, let go and collapsed with an awe-inspiring slowness before their eyes, the little group ran back along the path, clutching each other and mouthing silent prayers of thankfulness for their safety. And as Aunt Lavinia's house gave a last, creaking moan and fell to meet the welcoming arms of the sea, the spirit of little Edward swooped out over the waves, like a new-born bird crying joy to the sun.